MW01596501

UNDER THE AMORAL BRIDGE

by

Gary A. Ballard

A Cyberpunk Novel

Originally told in Serial Blog Form

amoralbridge.blogspot.com

Introduction

The book you hold in your hand is the unintended result of over 15 years of thinking, reading, and writing. The character of Artemis Bridge and his cast of supporting characters is a latecomer to the party. At first, he was meant to function as his namesake – a bridging character whose adventures set the stage for the novel I've been trying to publish since around 2005. That original series of novels which I started writing in 2001 was the main attraction. Bridge was a way for me to promote my writing online, to get my name *out there* to hopefully influential people who might one day want to pay me for that original series of novels. But in writing *Under the Amoral Bridge*, I found that I really dug the character of Artemis Bridge. He was a complete bastard, someone I could never sympathize with and could never like. But he was a great character to write. And before finishing this novel, two other novels started to write themselves in the back of my mind. Once I'd had some resting time, I began work on the second Bridge novel, which has just been completed and fully published online as *The Know Circuit*, found at http://amoralbridge.blogspot.com. The three novels, supporting short stories and GlobalPedia pieces all form the tapestry I call *The Bridge Chronicles*.

Publishing the novel serially on a blog was an idea I'd toyed with before, and it's helped me tremendously. I write more because no matter how few or how many hits the site gets, I feel an obligation to get that piece out there because someone might actually want to read it. Though I missed a few deadlines with *Under*, I'm happy to say that I didn't miss a day with *The Know Circuit*'s publishing schedule. Now that it's done, I intend to write the third chapter in the sequence and publish it online in the same manner as the previous two. In the interim, I will be writing at least one other Bridge short story and some supporting pieces, most of which will go online at the aforementioned web site to keep people interested.

But if the contents of this book and the sequel are available for free online, why am I self-publishing this physical edition? The most obvious reason is that I'd like to get paid for my work. It was over six months of my life, after all. Secondly, my hope is that more people will read a story of this size in a physical (or eBook) version than they will in chopped up bits on a blog. To give the non-free versions some added value, I've included an unpublished Bridge short story as a bonus. The story *Feeding Autonomy* will not appear on the web site or in a free version for the foreseeable future. Shortly before the third novel is published online, I plan to release *The Know Circuit* in a similar physical edition, and it will also include an unpublished Bridge short story.

Regular viewers of the web site (amoralbridge.blogspot.com) will be treated to additional material that is not available in print, such as GlobalPedia 2028. These pieces are meant to give some additional history to the world. News related to the Bridge series will also be posted to that site, as well as my personal blog at gameangst.blogspot.com. It's important to me that I give every channel something unique, my way of rewarding the people who become fans of *The Bridge Chronicles*.

And what about that original unpublished series? It's still out there, waiting to be rewritten in light of changes to the setting I've made in *The Bridge Chroni-*

cles. Many of the important historical events of that series are the central focus of the Bridge novels. At least two characters besides Bridge are integral to the second series. Whether that series will be published the same way as the Bridge novels is dependent on the success of this publishing model. Stay tuned to the web site in the future. When I know, you'll know.

So, I kept the introduction to less than 1,000 words, and you're probably ready for that Bridge fellow to take over. Thank you from the bottom of my heart for your purchase of this book. I hope you enjoy it.

Dedicated to my beloved wife

For all the support, love and understanding

Chapter 1
August 28, 2028
11:42 p.m.

"I know a guy," were the only important words Artemis Bridge uttered these days. All of his conversations with those words were a carefully choreographed dance routine, each step planned out in advance with only rare deviations from his expectations. Before those words came the usual bullshit, the greetings, the give and get probing Bridge used to determine if the prospective client was a cop trying to entrap him or a legitimate person with an illegitimate need. After those words, the dance was all details, the who-is and the where-wills and all the rest of the important minutiae that would get the job done. But "I know a guy," those were the focal point of Bridge's life. Those words were the music that drove the dance.

Bridge didn't yet know the well-dressed man coming across the Glitter bar towards him, but he could read the guy like a web site from the moment the sharp-dresser had entered the club. Bridge thought, 'Here's a guy that gets a little action on the side, a little weird action his girlfriend or wife won't give him. He's some well-heeled corporate douchebag looking for someone to help him exploit something.' The man's bearing was all faux confidence. His suit was Armani, his job was corporate, but his bravado was a subtly tarnished facade. Bridge pegged the client at around 32, desperately hoping he was still as cool as he was in high school, but deep down all too aware that the young things gyrating wildly in the club around him had moved on to more interesting predators. He was not cool, he was not crunk, he wasn't even hip and he sure wasn't cyber. He ogled the pretty

1

girls as he straightened his silk tie uncomfortably, his eyes shifting nervously from one younger alpha male to the next as he gestured for the bartender's attention. The man's eyes never held anything for long, except for constant predatory stares at any young female that happened by. He seemed especially interested in the girls with the cybernetic replacement limbs. 'Must have a metal fetish,' thought Bridge. The bartender directed the client over towards Bridge's table with an indifferent shrug, signaling at Bridge as the client turned his back. Costello the bartender was a stand-up guy who vetted prospective clients. All he ever asked for was a bit of hard-to-get '70's porn. Bridge knew a guy.

Sharp-Dressed stuck out a hand to Bridge as he approached the table, offering a handshake of dubious merit. Bridge waved off the proffered hand. "Sorry, I don't do physical contact," Bridge apologized. "There's too many crazy things can be transferred by touch in this business." Sharp-Dressed sat down quickly with a slightly offended expression, his eyes darting nervously as he straightened his jacket.

Bridge's paranoia excuse was a valid one. The people he dealt with were often lying shitheels of the worst kind. There were nanotech listening devices that could be planted through skin-to-skin contact, contact poisons and diseases of varying lethality, and portable weapons bladed and concussive that would make perfect tools of revenge. Bridge always tried to be fair in his dealings, but that never stopped unsatisfied customers from seeking recompense of a physical nature. But those weren't the reason he avoided physical contact. No, the real reason was that he just hated people on an almost universal basis. He hated the cloying press of humanity, the parade of simpering mongoloids that walked the face of the earth as if they owned it. He hated them for their greed, he hated them for their vices, and he hated their sweating, stinky desperation which fell off of them in waves no matter the circumstance. He hated Mr. Sharp-Dressed man here, for whatever connection this well-heeled faker wanted from Bridge.

Bridge wondered how Sharp-Dressed managed to not sweat his balls off in the intense Los Angeles heat outside, but the man showed only a thin line of perspiration on his brow. "You got a business card?" was the first question Bridge asked him. In any other environment, Bridge reckoned the man would have whipped out the bizchip before their handshake was even cold, but the potential illegality of the situation had obviously put the guy off personal revelations.

"Of course," Sharp-Dressed answered, whipping out a small card wallet from his breast pocket. He hesitated as the chip left his pocket, wondering if he really should be handing over his particulars to someone who could link him to a crime. "Isn't this business usually anonymous? No names and all that business?"

"Do you do business with a motherfucker won't tell you his name?"

Sharp-Dressed had a good think about that, finally handing over the card with only a slight reluctance tugging at the corners of his smile. The paper-thin silicon wafer glowed with exposure to the pulsating light show of the club, an animated presentation complete with video of the card's owner flashing boldly from the card's electronic paper surface. The man oozed oily confidence even from the bizchip.

"Your business with me is as secret as your confession," Bridge continued as he eyed the card. "You already know my name. We're just evening up the deal." Of course, Bridge was lying. Anonymity was a buzzword of his, but it wasn't religion

3

in his line of work. Bridge's first priority was protecting his own ass, and if that meant he had to "know a guy" he worked for when someone else asked, like a frisky cop or a mean big bastard with a big bastard gun, he'd sing like a canary. Knowing guys meant knowing their dirty little secrets, and he could trade secrets as well as connections when the need arose. "Good to meet you, Brandon Thames, Film Distribution Assistant," Bridge read from the card. "Are you a cop?"

Thames appeared taken aback, his affected calm showing signs of wear. "Boy, you don't waste any time. I like that, I dig that. No, I am not a cop. I'm not wearing any kind of wire or listening device." He manufactured a smile for Bridge, a smile filled with the ivory produce of a very expensive dentist and the cloying charm of a social predator. He opened his coat to display a crisply-laundered white shirt, as if that would allay all Bridge's fears.

"Wasting time is a sin in this business, and spending time in jail for what I do is a serious waste of time," Bridge replied.

"And what do you do, exactly?"

"I am my name. Artemis Bridge, pleasure to meet you. I'm a bridge, THE bridge, the path to whatever it is you want, so long as what you want is something hard to find that someone else has. It may be rare, it may even be illegal, but if you need it, I am the guy that knows the guy that's got it or does it. I'm the main circuit in the relationship network, I'm the go-between and the get-to-know. You stand here on one side of the bridge with a need, and somewhere on the other side of the bridge is the guy who can fulfill that need. For a nominal fee, I connect you with him. I do not touch the goods. I do not care what the goods are, whether it's information or mineral, virtual or physical. What you trade with the people I set you up

4

with is your business so long as my fee is paid." The well-rehearsed speech flowed from Bridge's lips like electricity through a wire.

"And you don't care what it is?"

"Not one iota. Couldn't give a rat's ass."

"Which is why they call you the Amoral Bridge."

"I'm surprised 'they' even know the meaning of the word amoral," Bridge quipped with a sarcastic smile. "It's an amoral shitstorm out there, Mr. Thames, and I'm just trying to keep dry."

"Can you guarantee confidentiality?"

"I'm still alive, aren't I? My clients are ghosts, Mr. Thames. The only people who will know you've done business with me are you and the person I introduce to you." Bridge lied, of course, neglecting to mention Aristotle, the six-foot-three lie watching from ten feet behind Bridge's left shoulder.

Aristotle was Bridge's bodyguard, a fantastically gigantic black man with biceps as thick as tree limbs and a stare that filled most with the fear of a black planet. Bridge had nicknamed him Aristotle during their interview last year, when the bodyguard had explained the philosophy of existentialism and how it related to the twenty-first century life under a corportocracy. Bridge hadn't understood a goddamn word of it, but it had sounded right. Bridge had decided at that point that Aristotle was a damn sight smarter than Bridge was, hiring him on the spot. Unfortunately, Bridge couldn't afford to pay him enough to actually engage in dangerous activities like fistfights. Bridge mainly kept him around for show, a bluff for the easily dissuaded, a bluff that succeeded more than it failed. The last ass beating Bridge was forced to take was eight months ago, and even Bridge would admit he had deserved it. Bridge glanced over Brandon's shoulder at the reflection of Aristotle in the mirrored walls, buttressing his confidence with the bodyguard's presence.

"So what is it you need? Women? Guns? Information?"

Thames voice fell into a hoarse whisper. "I need a leaker."

Bridge laughed a little on the inside. Every movie studio in the States had been conducting legal and not-so-legal wars against what they called intellectual piracy for decades. It had started with lawsuits in the late '90's, suing whatever poor soul they could drum up who had downloaded a copy of a movie or a song before its release date. As the corporations had gotten more legal power in the 2k's, their rhetoric about the effects of piracy on their business had gotten more zealous, and the legal wiggle room to protect their copyrights had expanded with the propaganda. By the early 2020's, many hackers spoke of hit teams who scoured the GlobalNet in search of anyone leaking books, games, movies, songs, software and TV shows. Net battles were fought, with rumors of the odd fatality here and there. And no matter how harsh the reaction, the hackers just kept leaking pirated goods and thumbing their noses at their corporate opposition.

But what few of the normal people not associated with either side knew was that the corporations hired people under the table to leak the releases. They had long ago discovered that pre-release buzz from legitimate reviewers and paid shills only generated so much interest in a media-saturated world. Unfiltered positive buzz from the hardcore underground, the pirates and the punks, was worth its weight in gold. As a result, the media corporations did what they did best. They made a deal. The corporate liaisons, like Brandon Thames here, would carelessly let the leaker know where and when to steal a copy of the media from the Global-Net database, like something 'falling off the truck' because the driver left the back door open. The hacker would still have to do the work, of course, breaking through security and reaching the prized goods. Like a virus, the stolen media would spread through the GlobalNet, building hopefully positive buzz that translated into bigger releases. The corporations got a boogieman to keep the average meathead from downloading leaked media, and the hackers got a little spending money and the infamy of making a big score. The system worked great, unless the product was a stinker, or the leaker got himself dead.

Bridge asked, "Have you ever worked with a leaker before?"

"All the time. My last guy got himself killed in some goddamn arena battle. That's the third one this year. I keep getting them from the temp pool of the collections department. Those credcrasher assholes are barely sober most of the time, and they all seem to have a death wish. I figured I'd see if you had a different talent pool to choose from."

Bridge put his chin in his palm for a moment, a practiced pantomime of thoughtful consideration. He couldn't think of anyone specific right off the top of his head, but Angela would. His brow furrowed, and he gave a desultory "Tsk!" before snapping his fingers. "I know a guy," he concluded.

"Great! When can I meet him?" Thames's face bled relief.

Bridge spread his hands in front of him. "Whoa, patience. I'll need to contact him and these guys don't exactly work a 9 to 5." He tapped Thames's business card to his forehead. "I'll give him your credentials and see if he's interested. If he is, I'll call you back and set up a meet. Be prepared, he's probably going to do a quick background search on you, make sure you're on the up and up, not a cop or anything."

"I told you, I'm not a cop," Brandon replied with a hint of irritation creeping into his voice. "CLED could bust me just as easily as him, after all. Technically, this is industrial espionage. It would make Chronosoft Entertainment look incredibly bad to the mouth-breathers out there."

Palms down on the table, Bridge calmed the angered executive. "Hey, I know you. We've sat here, we've shared some polite conversation and felt each other up. I know you're not a cop. HE won't know you're not a cop. I don't know what kind of yahoos you're used to dealing with, but real leakers are paranoid bastards. Good leakers get targeted by one of your little hit squads, so you can understand why he might want to be exceedingly careful." Bridge noted that Aristotle's attention had focused more intently on Bridge's back as the client's agitation had bubbled to the surface. Bridge gave him a subtle signal that things were fine. "Now, about my fee."

"Upon completion of the first successful leak, we'll deposit ten thousand in a non-traceable cash account at the vendor you specify."

"None of that corporate scrip or new federal bills with the tracking software," Bridge added. "I only deal in Five-Year." Bridge always insisted on "Five-Year," a term given to cash minted before 2023. That was the last year cash was produced without embedded chips that could trace every use of the currency as if it was a debit or credit card. Corporate scrip was issued by the company with the Local Government License or LGL, and was just as traceable. Chronosoft, besides employing Thames in the movie business, controlled the LGL for all of Los Angeles

County. Bridge wanted to steer well clear of their accountants, not to mention the IRS. There was no tax form for the self-employed whose only skill was "knowing guys."

"Once we have a deal, I'll give you the name of my exchange vendor. How soon will you want the first release?"

Thames practically jumped from his seat, reaching into his pocket. Aristotle leapt into action immediately, angling to support Bridge if need be. The businessman pulled out a flier, oblivious to the threat signals he was broadcasting. "The name of the movie is..."

Bridge cut him off with a quick wave of his hand. "Whoa, whoa, I don't want to know. The particulars are between you and your boy. The less I know the better." With a deflated expression, Thames replaced the flier in his pocket quickly. "All I need to know is how quickly do you need someone?"

"This needs to start going out in three days."

Bridge grimaced and sighed. "That's one tight deadline. I may not be able to get my top guy with that kind of turnaround. Have you thought about not waiting until nutcrunching time to try to pull this off?"

"I told you, my guy got whacked. I thought I had it taken care of. Will your guy be able to do it?"

"I said he wouldn't be the best, not that he'd be a muppet. Leaks are mostly cake and coffee runs, and the guys I know aren't fuckups. He'll take care of you."

Thames appeared pacified, finally attending to the drink he'd been fingering since he sat down. He downed the martini in one go, finishing it off by devouring the olive and depositing the toothpick into the glass with a brittle ting. "If that's all then, there's a girl at the end of the bar who's been dying for me to buy her a drink." His smile was all frat boy bravado, an unbecoming salaciousness reawakening his natural machismo. Bridge dismissed him with a playful shrug of his shoulders, pointing the man to the dance floor. Thames took off like an unleashed dog in heat.

Bridge sat back and let the music wash over him. It was forgettable for all its pomp, a mediocre example of the prograsmic genre. Made by programmers, prograsmic was a collage-like blend of old techno, rock and bits of random sound bites fashioned into songs not by hand, but by programs. Bits and bytes of code pieced it all together into a structure that sounded musical. But there was always something off about the compositions, at least to Bridge's untrained ear. One of his acquaintances had tried to explain it to Bridge with little success. The music followed the rules of traditional musical structures handed down through centuries of musical evolution, from the time man had started banging two rocks together and dug the rhythm. But the programs messed with that structure, focusing on agitating unconscious associations the mind made with certain notes and frequencies and beats, producing a feeling in some not unlike light drug use. It just made Bridge antsy.

Bridge's concentration was broken by Aristotle's voice cutting through the music. His bodyguard's voice was soft, yet forceful, the voice of someone assured of their power without a hint of overconfidence. "Your presence is being requested," Aristotle said matter-of-factly, his finger pointing across the club at the waving figure of Barney. Barney was a pain in the ass, one of the many ignorant gophers used by local mob shitheel Nicky Sharver.

"Fuck, that is just what I need," Bridge grumbled. One of Nicky's boys motioning to Bridge was never a good omen. It usually meant Nicky wanted something, and when Nicky wanted something, he didn't take no for an answer. Bridge gave a sarcastic smile and returned Barney's wave, mumbling under his breath, "Yeah, I see you, you ignorant cocksucker. Run along and tell your boss I'll be there soon." Barney pointed to the side exit, which led to the alleyway outside.

"He wants you in the alley," Aristotle said. "You know what that means."

"Yep. I'm about to get a beatdown. Did I piss him off this month?" Aristotle shrugged.

"We could go out the front, put him off until a more opportune time," the bodyguard offered.

"He'd just look for me until he found me somewhere else," Bridge replied, straightening his jacket as he stood. "Fuck it, the sooner I get this over with, the sooner I can get with Angela and get paid."

"You could always give me a raise and I'll deal with them," Aristotle said with a malicious smile.

"I can barely afford you now, mountain man. I'm not paying the ER doc to pull their teeth out of your knuckles. How do I look?" Bridge posed before the bodyguard, his clothes immaculate, his demeanor that of the condemned man. He gingerly fussed with his spiky black hair in the wall-length mirror. No sense looking like a mutt until after the violence.

"Like a man about to get his face smacked in," Aristotle joked. Bridge returned his smirk.

"Funny. Off to the gallows!" Bridge shouted, striding purposefully across the packed house to his inevitable beating.

Chapter 2
August 29, 2028
12:14 a.m.

Bridge made his way across the dance floor with a false air of confidence. He couldn't afford to let the plebes who might actually be paying attention think he wasn't in control. Dodging flailing arms and grinding hips, he was reassured that most were ignoring him completely, engrossed by their drunken mating dance. Halfway across the floor, he was stopped by a high-pitched squeal. "Bridge! Oh my God! Where have you been?" Even over the music, he could hear her voice. It was a keening wail he'd never wanted to hear again.

"Lola!" Bridge only just succeeded in sounding excited to see her. Her body slammed into his, her arms crushing his neck in a forceful hug that drove the air out of his lungs audibly. "What... what are you doing here?"

"Dancing, silly!" she screamed, jiggling her hips provocatively. Lola was an average beauty, the kind of barely pretty face that dreamed of lighting up the Global-Net in movies and films. She unfortunately lacked the charisma, acting skills and perfection of form that would have given her even half a chance. It never stopped her from trying, of course, but it had been many years of fruitless attempts, marred by countless exploitations. Bridge knew she was never going to make it. Her voice alone could wilt erections. "I never heard from you! Did you show that producer guy my disc?"

Not all of Bridge's transactions involved money, and Bridge had collected his fee from Lola without ever following through on his end of the unspoken bargain. She was the perfect mixture of unfulfilled desire and lackluster intelligence that made taking advantage so simple. Code words like producer, screen tests and lunch dates were all it took to unlock her resistance. Now Bridge had to think fast. "You know, I did, and he's supposed to get back with me when his schedule clears. He's knee-deep in a project right now."

She pointed at him, her eyes squinting as she smiled with a drunken mirth. "You're not lying to me, are you? You really showed it to him?"

Bridge pointed at his chest. "Would I lie? You can stand on me."

Leaning over with lustful intent, she breathlessly cooed, "Oooooo, Bridgie! And he liked it?" Bridge lied again with a nod. "You want another audition, baby?" Her breath was thick with alcohol. Bridge could just imagine Aristotle smirking behind him. He turned her around and extricated himself from her cloying grasp as delicately as he could.

"Another time, baby, I've got business to attend to. I'll call you." With that lie, he was away, his eye locked on Barney, ignoring the hurt expression darkening her features. 'The things I do for guilt-free sex,' he thought.

Barney was mumbling something as he opened the door to the alleyway, but Bridge couldn't hear it over the awful music that engulfed the club's interior. A sickly orange light flooded into the club through the open doorway, almost painfully bright in contrast to the flashing darkness of the interior. Bridge rubbed his eyes as he crossed the threshold, a piercing headache beginning behind his eyes as his pulse quickened in dread of the coming violence.

"Nicky said you gotta come quick, Bridge," Barney muttered. Like most hard cases, he went by a wholly unflattering nickname not of his choosing. Bridge wasn't sure what his given name was, but everyone called him Barney because his nasally voice bore an unfortunate resemblance to the purple dinosaur from a childhood TV show. Bridge had only seen the show on some backwater GlobalNet site after Nicky told him the origin of the nickname, but the comparison was hilariously apt. His gangly form and mopey eyes didn't help matters.

"I'm coming, Barney, I'm coming," Bridge replied irritably. He looked down at his feet to acclimate his eyes to the changing light. It wasn't that the alley was overly bright, but his eyes always adjusted slowly. The fact that he slept such weird hours never helped. He cursed under his breath at a flier that had gotten stuck to his shoe. The alley was full of them, glossy political fliers with embedded video, stumping for the upcoming Los Angeles mayoral race. Bridge peeled the flier off with his other foot, spitting on the video of the current asshole in charge, Oliver Sunderland. Bridge didn't have much respect for any politicians, but that grinning bastard earned Bridge's special contempt for being a corporate-appointed shill.

Last year had been a nightmare year for America in general, but particularly for Los Angeles. The United States government had gone bankrupt in late 2026. Bridge didn't understand all the talking head blather about how a government that printed its own money could go bankrupt but the effect was clear. The government had no money, which meant the state of California had no money, and the city in turn had no money. The politicians in Washington had spent 2026 bickering with their thumbs up their asses instead of figuring out how to fix the problem, while the states and cities suffered. Los Angeles was a picture of what Aristotle called class inequity in still life, upper crust assholes with gold-plated swimming pools and gated communities living blocks from drug-infested shitholes where the poor shot each other over neckbones. Bridge lived among the shit-upon, the people who relied on food stamps and free clinics to live something close to a normal life. First the government food dried up and then the free clinics closed. City workers were sent home without pay. Crime skyrocketed as people got desperate, and the cops who hadn't been laid off to cut costs started walking off the job when their paychecks stopped coming. Riots followed hunger like thunder follows lightning.

Then along come the corporations. Congress signed the Local Governance License Act of 2027, and suddenly megacorporations like Chronosoft were allowed to bid for Local Governance Licenses, or LGL's. The government handed civil administration of Los Angeles to Chronosoft for a song. They established Chronosoft Law Enforcement Division or CLED, who were much better at policing Bridge's information trade than LAPD. Their board of directors appointed a city council with Sunderland as mayor. The LGL was allowed to run for one year with appointed officials, and that year was up. Elections were four days away, and based on the number of Sunderland fliers in the alleyway, he was trying damned hard to keep his LGL gravy train rolling.

Bridge held the whole LGL scheme in contempt. It was bad enough when giant corporations paid lobbyists to pillage the country legally, even worse when the government gave them control over virtual city-states. CLED's efficiency led Bridge to change illicit careers. Information theft was a definite crime, but now Bridge worked in a grey area of legality. That didn't stop most CLED officers from trying to squeeze him for information but as long as he didn't touch any of the goods, they had no real legal leverage over him. That left many of them to use extralegal leverage. LAPD had been easy to deal with in comparison. Grease the right palms with a pittance and you were golden. It wasn't as if the cops had been paid worth shit, so any extra income was welcomed by all but the hardcore crusaders. CLED, on the other hand, paid their officers handsomely and gave them carte blanche to actually enforce whatever laws Sunderland's government laid down. Bridge couldn't afford to bribe CLED officers, he had to finesse them.

Bridge started to complain, "Now what is so important..." but he never finished the sentence. Caught in mid-stride by a punch to the gut, he doubled over with a loud exhalation. One of Nicky's boys had come from behind the dumpster to the left while Bridge was distracted by the flier, delivering a blow that left him gasping for air. He managed to stay on his feet, but only by leaning on the dumpster. Three more men surrounded him, their shadows growing long over the slick ground. Last night's rain had pooled in the alley, and the humidity still hung in the air, causing Bridge's back to break out in a thin line of sweat. Bridge gasped, "I assume there's a problem?"

"You goddamn right, dere's a problem!" Nicky shouted from over Bridge's right shoulder. Bridge heard Nicky's pimp cane tapping the pavement, and there he was, dressed in the finest white Egyptian cotton suit, a purple and gold tie setting off the stark whiteness of the suit with almost painful intensity, fat cheeks pouring over the coat's high collar. Nicky never could let go of his LSU roots, garish "Geaux Tigers" colors queering up what would otherwise be acceptable fashion sense. "We got a big fucking problem dere."

"I'm sure we can discuss it rationally like two grown men," Bridge responded, finally able to stand his full six feet again. He spared a glance at Aristotle, who stood with arms folded trying to look mean and succeeding. A few of Nicky's guys were eyeing his stance nervously. They weren't used to fighting people with the ability to fight back, but Aristotle's non-threatening body language confused their limited intelligence.

"No, we done passed the point of rational men, Bridge. You set me up a doser."

Bridge thought back over his recent dealings with Nicky. He would much rather never know a guy like Nicky, but in his business, pickiness was not an option.

The transplanted Cajun ran a crew of thieves and leg-breakers, passing money up the chain of organized crime to people with much more juice. He was just as likely to steal goods from shipping trucks as he was to steal credit information from GlobalNet accounts, and never without a healthy dose of needless violence. Where other criminals were elegant, Nicky was a rabid dog. He liked hurting people. Bridge had set him up with a hacker, a generally reliable scrub named Z@m@, for some big heist Nicky had planned. "Z@m@'s clean, Nicky. He swore to me he was clean."

"He coulda swore he was the Queen of Fuckin' England, and he still woulda been lying. He got nicked selling a month's worth of Trip to undercover CLED. Now he's doing a dime upstate and I got no hacker." Nicky leaned angrily on the cane. "So I'm taking it out of yo' ass." He nodded tersely to his crew, but they hesitated, eyes glued to the giant bodyguard. Nicky cocked his head, eyeing Aristotle with a petulant squint. "We gonna have an issue with dat, big man?"

Aristotle shook his head, his hands held out in front of him in a gesture of peace. "I don't pay him enough to sully his hands on your boys," Bridge quipped with a resigned sigh.

"Maybe you oughtta t'ink 'bout dat dere," Nicky snickered. "Might save you a few teeth."

"I got expenses. Just don't bust my face too much. Clients don't react well to black eyes." The crew started to close in on Bridge. He raised his hands for one final plea. "Look, what can I do to make this up? I didn't know he was on Trip. Hell, half of these guys are on it 24/7 and you'd never know it. Most of 'em claim it makes them better crackers. I can get you another guy!"

"Oh, you gon' do dat, sucker. But I can't just let you off with a warning. You got to pay a fee for my time and trouble, or else da' community gon' t'ink I'm weak." The first blow caught Bridge across the back of his legs, bringing him down to his knees in a puddle with a splashy thud. It felt like a bat or a club. A boot landed squarely in his breadbasket, sending the air rushing out of his body again. A fist across his jaw made him angry.

"FUCK, Joey, I told you not the face!" Bridge mumbled over a swelling jaw. He spit a bloody mess on the ground.

"Sorry, Bridge," Joey offered with a sheepish grin. Bridge had hooked him up with a digital pimp that provided virtual ageplay scenarios. Joey liked the jailbait, but Nicky frowned on his boys cruising the high schools, so cyberbait was the solution. Another shot with the club across Bridge's back put his face on the ground, a wet, gritty mess sticking to his clean-shaven cheek.

The blows came in slow, measured succession. They weren't really trying to damage him, just make it hurt while having a bit of fun. Each hardguy took a turn, planting a kick in his ribs or a punch to his gut. The blows started to merge into one series of painful flashes when he heard one of his attackers scream out in pain. The beating ceased, the shuffle of feet replacing the sickening thuds of fists on flesh.

"What the hell's going on here?" yelled a female voice infused with a steel-edged air of authority. It took Bridge a moment to recover his senses enough to recognize the voice. Silence followed her initial question. "I asked you what's going on here. Now am I going to get an answer or do I have to haul you all in?"

Bridge opened his eyes and peered up at Gina Danton, CLED hardass. Danton stood about 6', her blonde hair pulled into a tight bun underneath the CLED cap. She was a looker, though Bridge always thought she was the kind who didn't know just how good she looked. She seemed more concerned with proving how big of a badass she could be. But unlike most of the assholes CLED had hired from the old LAPD ranks, Danton was fair. She wasn't out to bust someone's ass just because she could. He was also never happier to see her in his life.

He spat a wad of bloody phlegm on the ground. "Officer Danton, you're looking lovely tonight."

"That's Patrolman Danton to you. Bridge, did I just interrupt a beatdown?" She offered a hand to the fallen man. "Stand up and stop staring at my ass." He grabbed her hand. She pulled him up with surprising strength.

"Me? A beatdown? Who would want to administer a beatdown to someone as charming and effervescent as me?" Bridge wobbled a bit but maintained his balance. "I merely slipped and fell into a pack of rabid alley rats, and these gentle-men were kind enough to chase them off of me. Rats are filthy bastards, you know, diseases and all."

"Uh huh," Danton replied. "That what happened, Aristotle?" The black man shrugged and nodded sheepishly.

"He's a rather maladroit bumbler," was all the bodyguard would say. Bridge huffed loudly, checking his body for significant damage. There appeared to be no breaks, but he was going to be bruised for a month.

She scoffed sourly. "That's how it's gonna be, then? Do I look stupid to you? How about you, boys? I look that stupid to you?"

Nicky put on his slimiest grin. "No, chere, you look like a lady deserves a fine meal and some sweet talkin'." He oozed. Bridge grinned painfully to himself. Trying that approach with her was likely to get Nicky a smack.

"Put it back in your pants, Casanova," Danton shot back. "I ain't one of your Barbie dolls. Why were your boys pounding on Bridge here?" Their silence infuriated her more. "Bridge, it doesn't have to go down like this. You say the word, and I'll haul 'em in for assault and battery. Go through their pockets, look for illegal guns, drugs, whatever."

"No charges, Patrolman Danton. It's all good." She scowled again.

Turning quickly on Sharver, her anger was a cool fist wrapped in iron. "Fine. You and your boys get the fuck out of here before I decide to search you just on GP. Do not let me see you around here again tonight." She emphasized the point with sharp jabs of her billy club towards Nicky.

"Nice ta meetcha, Patrolman Danton," Nicky said with a shark-toothed grin. "Bridge, we'll speak another time." His boys formed a cordon surrounding him as they walked out of the alley.

"What the fuck was that about, Bridge?" Danton spat as she whirled on Bridge. "I could have had him up on enough to give me a warrant on his place. And we both know that would have turned up a gold mine."

Bridge knew it all too well. He knew that she was too honest to trump up a reason to search Nicky's place by planting evidence. And Bridge knew that if Nicky did get nicked because of a beatdown on Bridge, tonight's beating would have just been a preamble to an epic, fatal orchestra of violence lasting weeks. No need to rock that boat. Bridge could handle a beatdown.

"You bust him, he gets someone to bust me a helluva lot worse. In the grand scheme of things, a little beatdown is a trivial cost of doing business."

"What business are you into with Nicky?" she asked, cop curiosity piqued.

Bridge grinned and wiped the blood from his lips. "Oh, Patrolman Danton, my lips are sealed. I know nothing, I see nothing, I hear nothing. I'm just a..."

"I know, you're just a bridge. Spare me, I've heard it before. See no, hear no, speak no evil. Next time he comes around looking to polish his knuckles with your face, I might not be around." Bridge just shrugged. "The offer's still open," she stated matter-of-factly.

The offer was a death sentence, if not in actuality, in the sense that her deal would end his way of life for good. She had tried to cultivate Bridge as a confidential informant for months, to drop dime for a pittance. CLED paid better than LAPD, but the principle was still the same. A rat was a rat was a rat, no matter how big that rat's payday.

He'd have been a gold mine for her, but he wasn't interested in being anyone's meal ticket but his own.

"That's a non-starter and you know it," Bridge replied. "I'm no rat."

"Then you better get used to those bruises."

"Already there."

"Maybe you should think about finally paying him enough to be an actual bodyguard," Danton said as she pointed to Aristotle. "Keep it clean, Bridge."

"I always do, Officer Danton."

"Patrolman Danton, goddamnit!" She waved behind her as she exited the alley.

Once out of earshot, Bridge said, "Let's get moving. I've got to find another hacker before Nicky gets his panties in a bunch again. Angela is not going to be happy to hear from me."

Chapter 3
August 29, 2028
1:20 a.m.

Bridge staggered into his apartment after seeing Aristotle off in a cab, figuring he wouldn't need a faux bodyguard for the walk up to his place. It was the kind of perfect shithole Los Angeles apartment made cliched in so many bad movies, a series of Spanish adobe-style buildings with too little attention paid to maintenance. He lived in a second floor apartment in the back of Celestial Gardens, close enough to the Central City area to hear the nightly gunshots, but far enough away to be out of the firing line. Most of the residents kept to themselves, especially when the police were busting the Trip labs that sprung up throughout the complex like mushrooms, and he liked it that way.

The apartment was a mess as usual. His neat dress was an agonizingly maintained illusion of impeccable style, but his natural inclination tended towards barely constrained chaos. Though he never kept food and trash and dirty dishes all over, he did tend to stack things in untidy piles, books and news faxes and snail mail all heaped in their own disorderly scheme. He rarely threw these types of things away, regardless of how outdated. Angela had kept the place even messier, as she was the type to just leave food out, like most of the hackers Bridge had ever known.

The thought of Angela brought his mind back to business. He hesitated to contact her, even though she was the person to call for information thieves. She ran a stable of freelance hackers, brokering their information like a pimp brokers whores. Angela was a damn skilled hacker in her own right, and that skill had got-ten her enough money to set up her network. Not that long ago, Bridge had been one of her dogs and more besides.

They'd met back in '26 when he was just an arrogant freelancer looking for a job. Angela had already been brokering for a year, and she saw talent in Bridge despite his careless swagger. Within six months of the first job, they'd fell into a GlobalNet relationship, just Netsex for the first few months before they ever met in the flesh. The first skin meet had ended in bed, where they stayed for a whole weekend, never even touching the crèche. Two months of that had them moving into this place together as an official couple. They were a formidable tandem on the GlobalNet, in a field dominated by solo acts. Life had been good, until the riots.

The 2027 food riots had started in mid-summer, egged on by the massive heat wave and the callous indifference of the federal budget crisis. When federal aid to the states disappeared, welfare food shipments disappeared and poor people starved. First, there was looting, then wholesale ransacking of government facili-ties and then it got really nasty. Police stations, already undermanned by those officers who wouldn't strike, were assaulted by well-organized mobs. Bridge and Angela hadn't given too shits, watching the news coverage of the violence from the safety of the crèche with bemused cynicism. So long as someone would brave the violence to deliver a pizza and their Net connection held up, he and Angela could have lasted indefinitely.

Once the mobs started taking down local switches and power grids because there was little else to destroy, the couple were forced into the open. Rather than watching dispassionately, they had to brave the mobs just to find food. Those two days had been an eternity, but seeing up close the gibbering screams of human beings dropped to the level of animal violence he'd never witnessed before had broken his spirit in ways he never expected. When the corporations stepped in to quell the riots, Bridge swore off the crèche completely. He wanted nothing more to do with that make-believe world of bits and bytes. Much to his surprise, the riots had unearthed an alarming penchant for manipulating all the worst desires of humanity to get what he needed. Rather than steal information, he found much more pleasure in aiding sleazy fuckers get together in some macabre dance of self-immolation, feeding their secret hungers for immorality while keeping himself distanced from the cesspool.

Angela did not take the abrupt career change well. She was no innocent, since brokering information was highly illegal no matter how many corporations availed themselves of her services.

But something about the slick persona, the impeccable fashion, and Bridge's adamant refusal to use a crèche again infuriated her. She retreated to the crèche more than usual, and all too soon they were living separate lives, unable or unwilling to cross the divide between them. Finally, she moved out, taking her crèche and what little physical property she still owned. Their mutual friends, the ones who would still talk to Bridge after the breakup, would tell him about her personal life every so often, whether he wanted to hear it or not. Though she had become a physical recluse and shunned most human contact, it hadn't stopped her from shacking up with some hacker who lived in Seoul. But she was still a great contact for Bridge, someone who could provide hackers like the one he needed now. Angela still trusted Bridge, at least as far as she trusted anyone in her business.

Bridge walked into the bedroom and past the night stand where the last picture they'd taken sat. He picked it up and stared at it forlornly for a moment, thinking of the day the picture had been taken. Before the riots, they'd gone to a New Year's Eve party in Boyle Heights. The hacker gang *Los Magos* rented a string of houses in the neighborhood, and they'd hosted their own block party. Bridge remembered that some poser hacker, Dark-something or other, had insisted that everyone at the party get a photo for some GlobalNet slideshow museum room. The guy got whacked soon after, so the slideshow was never built, but Bridge finagled a download and put it by their bed. Angela had laughed, calling him a soppy sentimental bitch, but Bridge liked the shot. They both looked drunk in the picture, Angela's seedy blonde hair matted with sweat, her skin shiny from the exertions of dancing and running from house to house. Angela wasn't what most would call beautiful. So much time in the crèche had turned her average looks into something else entirely, skin pale and yellowed, eyes a little too sunken. She had put on makeup that night, though, and to Bridge, she had been about as pretty as a girl could get. He had drunk a great deal that night, and his memories might have beer goggles. Even after all the bitterness and fighting, she was still beautiful to his eyes.

Bridge set aside the memory with only a little pang and steeled himself for the coming conversation. It never went well, even when both agreed amicably on the business at hand. There would be cutting remarks, remarks that often led to retreading old arguments if either was in a mood. 'Just get the business done,' he told himself. He sat next to the neglected crèche.

The pill-shaped device, used to connect to the GlobalNet in the most visceral way possible, was covered in a thin shroud of dust, dulling the normally shiny surface. He ran a finger through the dust, letting out an exasperated sigh as he rubbed the greasy film between his thumb and forefinger. Proximity to the device tempted him, a muted siren's call to undress, open the coffin-like lid and climb into the lukewarm saline solution, to plug his interface jack in, sheathe his genitals in the waste catch and sink down into the glorious rush of jacking in. He missed the free-fall adrenaline of consciousness translated into pure data, of his body rendered in liquid mercury, shifting and changing with his every thought. He missed the thrill of cracking databank security, of running from anti-intrusion software and other hackers.

But those days were done. He bent over and opened the panel on the bottom of the crèche for remote access. Bridge pulled the interface plug out, dragging it back to the interface jack on the back of his neck and plugged in.

Remote access to the GlobalNet was nothing like crèche work. There was still the rush of dissolution, the feeling of consciousness disintegrating and then the re-emergence of sensory perceptions as Bridge's netbody rezzed into the crèche's entry room. But compared to crèche work, his NetBody was mired in mud, a sloppy, dragging sensation of lethargy encapsulating his actions. Sensory input that was normally sharper than real life was dull and uninteresting with remote access. It made him miss crèche work that much more.

Putting aside his desire, Bridge surveyed his entry room. Decorated with a baroque theme, like an 18th century Parisian ballroom, it gave Bridge a surge of pride. He had done all the texture work himself. Unfortunately, the textures were at least a generation behind what the latest crèche's could handle, and to his critical eye, the whole room now felt outdated. But it wasn't as if he entertained there anymore. He sat down in a lush, almost throne-like chair and accessed the room's external communications menu, sending Angela a request for direct entry into one of her chats. Fiddling with a useless puzzle game in a floating window while he waited, he was surprised at how fast the response came. He grabbed hold of the floating key, which dragged him bodily through a hole in the air, depositing him in an elaborately-decorated room in the blink of a virtual eye.

Angela's chat rooms always tended towards the fanciful, leaning heavily on a lack of gravity, objects floating by for no apparent reason. She'd always said, "If I want gravity, I'll go walk around the goddamn park." Bridge rezzed in upside down, though the concepts of up or down were purely perceptual and ineffective for describing his position relative to the rest of the room. If he had a stomach, it would have turned. His inner eyes adjusted to the whacked out perspective, and he began to examine the décor. The backdrop was space, an inky black cloud broken up by twinkling stars with the occasional brightly-colored galactic cloud. Bridge on his throne floated among a constellation of miniature cities, each covered in a shiny dome. Closer inspection revealed that each city was populated by a tiny civilization. He recognized the architecture of one of the cities as a virtual playground Angela ran for fun. All those tiny people were other real people on the GlobalNet, playing out their fantasies on worlds he presided over like a god.

"Do you like my little experiments?" Angela said with a bubbly giggle in her voice.

"I didn't realize this was your admin interface," Bridge replied. He examined the city he'd known as Ars-Perthnia more closely. He began to recognize landmarks that'd he only seen from street level with a fascinated rubbing of his chin. "Blows my mind."

"It wasn't always like this. I just added it last week. I got the idea after a 4-night run without any sleep. I was seeing some REAL strange shit." She began to giggle in that mischievous, snorting sort of way she always had when a devious idea hit her. "It's like I'm watching all my little minions running around doing minion shit in my little Dyson spheres."

Her NetBody was gorgeous as always. Tall, lithe and graceful, she took on the perfect model of an undead liche queen, a white-skinned dark goddess. She rarely ever let her real looks influence her avatar's appearance. He imagined her real face, with crooked teeth and sleep-deprived eyes but with a cuteness that shined through her average looks. Her self-image of the physical was terrible, but her NetBody was frighteningly gorgeous. He would always tell her how beautiful she was, but she insisted on obsessing over what she perceived as her physical flaws. Seeing her NetBody now brought back all the old feelings again, a pang of loss doing a drive-by on his heart.

"Is that Perthnia?"

"Yep. Bet you never saw it from this angle. Your old buddy Cyndal is running his own guild now." A picture of Cyndal's Hierdul avatar popped up beside Angela, his stern look daring the viewer to start something. Cyndal was always a right ass-hole. "I've already had like 17 complaints against them and it's only been two weeks since he quit Crimson Swords. Wanna fuck with their raid?"

Bridge waved his hands in front of his chest. "I've gotta get some sleep after this. I've got at least three meetings tomorrow night. I just needed a favor."

"Meetings. Fleshy meetings?" Bridge nodded. Angela's face took on an evil scowl. "You're still schmoozing and boozing, huh? Who you meeting with? Some pedo wants a guilt-free childplay avatar? You can cater to the kid diddlers in here, then brain blast them when you feel like it."

"That was the one time, and the guy only bought avatars and AI," he lied. There were a surprising number of guys looking for custom ageplay avatars. "At least he wasn't out raping real kids and shit."

"That you know of. You don't think he'll get tired of the virtual shit eventually and get him some fresh meat?"

Bridge sighed. This was such an old argument. "Not my problem. He needed something. I set him up with someone who could fill that need. I never touched any of it."

"You amoral fucker."

"Rent don't pay itself. You'd rather I go knock over old ladies' pension funds, or become one of those cred-crashing fucks for some faceless corp? It's not like I'm doing any of the things these shitheels ask me for." He stopped himself on the edge of a rant, putting his hands defiantly on his knees. "I'm here for business, ba... Angie." He had to refrain from calling her 'baby.' Those times were over.

She raised a finger as if to continue the argument, then snapped her mouth shut on the words. "Fine. What do you need?" Each word was a swirling blizzard, sharply clipped and full of venom, made all the more frigid by the addition of a reverb filter on her voice.

"Just a leaker, but I need him sharpish. Like tomorrow at the latest. Working a tight deadline. And he can't be one of those goddamn trippers you use. The client doesn't want druggies and arena adrenaline junkies."

"Coffee and cake runner. Sure, I got a guy." She leafed through a few files, and tossed one to Bridge, which floated into his hands as a streaking comet.

"Lil' Kira."

"Kira? Woman?" Angela shook her head. "He's not one of those gender-confused hormone-overloaded psychos, is he?"

"No, the name is short for Akira. Loves the old school manga and shit. He's always a bit jumpy, but he's solid. Never bottled on a job. Where you want to meet him?"

Bridge thought it over for a second, analyzing his schedule in floating window. "I'll be at the Arsenal between nine and midnight, maybe one o'clock. He can get me there."

"The Arsenal? That soccer club on Wilshire? They'll never let him in a place that upscale."

"If he can't get in, just have him send a bouncer in after me. I'll have 'em looking out for me. They all know me."

Angela paused for a minute, something obviously on her mind. "I still got a spot for you on my crew, babe. You can go back to running, if you want. It ain't the same without you."

"I thought you had Kim." An acid reply.

"Yeah, he's great but he's in Seoul. Sometimes I could use a little fleshy cuddling."

"Good night, Angie. Thanks for the help. Have fun with the spheres." He quickly jacked out without waiting for a reply. He'd probably hear about it the next time they spoke, but for now he just wanted to get some sleep. It was already close to three a.m.

Sleep wouldn't come. He spent hours tossing and turning, rolling in memories, before giving up and heading to the couch. He flipped on the GlobalNet vids, browsing through channel after channel of fare from infomercials to interactive shows to late-night porn and the big net news. One commercial caught his eye, for a new sitcom coming in the fall. Called Misogynist Theatre, the 30-second spot stopped Bridge's browsing dead in his tracks, if for no other reason than the buxom brunette flouncing around onscreen. "Nothing like a great pair of breasts to grab your attention," he muttered to himself. Once the commercial had finished, he used the remote to schedule a recording of the show. He also sent out an AI agent to search for some pre-release leak versions of the premiere. Two months out was enough lead-time for the leakers.

The next commercial made him shut the vids off in disgust. It was yet another political ad for the mayor's race, this one for the challenger, Arturo Soto. Soto was an attractive Hispanic man, slick and suave and the complete opposite physically of the more corpulent Caucasian Sunderland. Bridge would be damn glad when the election was finished. It was only four... no three days away now, this upcoming Saturday. "Fucking politicians," he muttered, stalking to the kitchen and grabbing the bottle of sleeping pills. The bottle was almost empty, so he cut one of the flimsy paper tabs in half and let it dissolve on his tongue. He wouldn't need a whole hit anyway. He had to get moving shortly after noon.

Unconsciousness found him soon after.

Chapter 4
August 29, 2028
6:33 p.m.

The Arsenal was one of the first new clubs built after the riots. A neon-saturated marvel of ultra modern design, it contained a separate dance club, concert hall, sports bar and the requisite VIP lounge upstairs. Awash in soccer brands and memorabilia, the club was lit by huge video screens showing live and archived game footage from around the world. Run by former L.A. Galaxy footballer Crispin Twiggs, the Arsenal acted as a front for prostitution, chip drugs and loan-sharking. Twiggs had been expelled from the game of soccer for gambling, but his public image had been somewhat rehabilitated by the outward success of the Arsenal. The vague whisperings of the club's illegal side businesses did not slow its trade in the slightest. It was the place to be.

Getting into the club regularly was difficult for those not already affiliated with professional soccer. The beautiful people were allowed in, of course, especially the celebrities and their hangers on. It was especially popular with the nouveau riche Latino celebrities that had come to be the face of the rebuilt Los Angeles. GlobalNet actors like Richie Delgado and tella novella divas like Anise Vargas were the face of the LGL's success. Bridge had worked for almost a month to get through the bouncers, until he finally found one who needed a connection with a black market cyberware doc. Bridge had hooked up Benny and Benny had returned the favor by giving him access to Twiggs. The Arsenal's initial success was illusory, and by its second month in business, Twiggs was up to his eyeballs in debt.

Bridge had given Twiggs the in with a new set of investors, the kind that wanted their investments kept quiet. Once Bridge had made that connection, he became a regular fixture, schmoozing his way into the VIP.

The night promised to be a busy one. The Arsenal always had its fair share of prospective clients, and Bridge was practically an unofficial employee. He knew the bartender's routines, their schedules, their likes and their guilty secrets. A night of fitful sleep had left him slightly off-kilter, the whole cab ride a dozy daze. Aristotle tried to engage him in conversation but took the hint when Bridge showed little interest in discussing the difference between determinism and existentialism, lapsing into an indifferent silence. Bridge hoped Angie's leaker showed up early. The thought of another beatdown from Nicky's boys was going to drive him to distraction until he'd taken care of the problem. He'd managed to cover up most of the bruises on his face with Skin in a Tube™, but the fat lip was a problem. Of course, knowing the Arsenal, the leaker wouldn't be allowed in. Hackers rarely showed great personal hygiene, and even less style, both of which were essential to mingle with the Arsenal's beautiful people. Bridge managed it with charm and wit and impeccable attire, despite his average looks.

The club was already packed, even at this early hour. Though not the only club on the street, it was certainly the most popular, with a line of supplicants running down the block waiting eagerly to be judged worthy by the bouncers. There were actually two entrances. One bouncer waved the regulars in through the front where the paparazzi could photo their grand entrances, while the uninitiated waited in a line running down the street. Most would wait in vain. Bridge made for the front entrance, flashing a smile at the bouncer. The bouncer stopped him cold with a meaty hand in Bridge's chest. "And just where do you think you're going, luv?" The bouncer's voice was thick with an urban British accent.

Bridge appraised the man. He was big. Not Aristotle big, much more of a lanky big, like a soccer player. The hand placed on Bridge's chest was strong. He didn't look like a bouncer, most of whom were gigantic slabs of beef. The face was rugged, with a crooked nose that indicated it had been broken at least once. "I was just going inside," Bridge replied with an amiable smile. "I've got business to discuss."

"Right now, your business is with me. Who are you, then?"

"Artemis Bridge, pleasure to meet you. And you?" Bridge offered up his best innocent smile. The bouncer's ape-like features wrinkled as he eyed the club's entry list on his cybernetic HUD.

"Don't see your name on the list, luv." His arms crossed over his chest in a defiant manner. Bridge spotted a familiar face over the bouncer's shoulder.

The bouncer working the newbie line was Stonewall Ricardo, someone Bridge had helped out a number of times. Ricardo had played soccer in Mexico before coming to the states to much fanfare in the early '20's. Known as a feared center half, he earned the nickname Stonewall for his physicality, his ability to stop an attack dead in its tracks. Stonewall's career had been ended early by a horrible knee injury requiring a cybernetic knee replacement. The league still banned the use of cybernetic replacements, and barred from the pitch, he had disappeared in disgust.

Twiggs had given Stonewall a job, but Bridge had always felt there was more between the two than just footballer camaraderie. Anytime Bridge asked about it,

Stonewall became as silent as his namesake. Bouncing was Stonewall's front job, but most of the time he was in charge of leg-breaking for Twiggs's other businesses. The footballer was the nicest guy you'd ever talk to, unless you were his target. Then all the anger and frustration of a man denied his passion would flow out onto the target with a homicidal fury. Luckily for Bridge, Stonewall had needed something he could never reveal to anyone but Bridge. Stonewall had needed therapy, from a shrink that wouldn't rat out his illegal activities to the cops or his criminal friends. Bridge knew a guy, the therapist to the shitheels, whose client list was as infamous as it was long. Ever since, Stonewall had Bridge's back.

Stonewall caught Bridge's predicament with a stray glance. Bridge waved to the bouncer, who was busily engaged with an average-looking blonde with horrific combat boots trying to beg her way in. With those boots, Bridge figured she had more chance of fitting through the eye of a needle than getting past the bouncers. Stonewall raised a finger to the girl and walked over to Bridge and the big side of beef blocking his entrance. "¿Qué onda? Is there a problem, Paulie?" he said to the bouncer, slipping between English and barrio Spanish with ease.

"Not a prob, guv. Just doing me job."

"This here's Bridge. Bridge, Paulie. Bridge here's a good friend of the club." Paulie raised a meaty eyebrow with an almost disgusted air.

"He ain't on me list," Paulie protested meekly. "If we's just gonna let anybody what ain't on the list in, what's the point of me?"

"Bridge's a special case. I'll take the heat if he causes trouble. Cool?"

Paulie seemed about to make some other argument before waving Bridge on through without further comment. Bridge tipped his nonexistent hat at the bounc-

37

er as he walked past with Stonewall in tow.

"Gotta forgive him, Bridge," Stonewall explained. "He's new and a bit of a *pendejo*, know what I mean? He supposedly knows Twiggs from somewhere, came begging for a job today. He ain't exactly making friends. Thinks 'cos he played in the Premiership, us MLS guys should just kiss his white English ass." He snorted disgustedly as he opened the glass door for Bridge. "You need anything tonight?"

"As a matter of fact, there's a guy may come looking for me. A hacker, so he's probably not going to be on the list, so to speak. If you can't let him in, just have him wait outside and send me a message, k? Think his name's Kira or eK1ra or some such idiotic combination of numbers and letters."

"Will do, Bridge." With that, he was in. Bridge noticed a flier for the band playing later in the evening, The Ardents. The walls along the entry hallway were decorated with football jerseys from around the world. Bridge noted authographed jerseys for Liverpool, Arsenal, Valencia, Boca Juniors, and of course, the L.A. Galaxy. The club opened up into subtly-partitioned enclosures, wide-open spaces broken by short walls and standing lamps. The interior design was stuffed with modern gadgetry. Each sub-space had its own white noise walls, separating and encapsulating the sounds of each area within its own space. The sports bar, with the live Galaxy match playing on gigantic screens was no louder than a quiet buzz, completely cut off aurally from the dance club which drowned in the sound of a booming prograsmic beat. The concert hall was on a similar auditory island, and each table in all areas had its own white-noise mask, hiding conversations in an invisible cloak from eavesdroppers while allowing in the area's particular attraction, whether it be the band, the dance beat or the game. Bridge knew that the VIP lounge upstairs was similarly equipped, with the ability to pipe first-floor audio to each table individually. The Arsenal was a stark contrast to a shithole club like the Glitter. It had the most expensive and exclusive technology designed to make the club the utmost in both privacy and public display.

The crowd was a mish mash of beautiful people and football fanatics. Everyone was dressed in their most fashionable couture, brand names flashing like Christmas decorations. Gaudy logos were the latest fashion trend. Every fashion designer seemed intent on signing his work in the most audacious possible manner. Dark fabrics clashed with insane combinations of low-tech glitter and thin-film video panels. Many were walking advertisements for their favorite fashion line, fetish or movie, their video panels a constant stream of GlobalNet messages that paid them a dividend for impressions, repetitions and click-thrus. Bridge worked his way through the crowd into the concert hall. The stage was set dead center in the room, a round dais surrounded by a small dance floor and tiers of tables placed in perfect staggered fashion so that no seat was visually or aurally obstructed from the action. The room reminded him of a miniature Vegas showroom. A video holograph was playing on the stage as Bridge walked in, a GlobalNet-transmitted performance from one of the virtual worlds playing in eerily-transparent pantomime. Bridge's table was as far from the door as he could manage. Aristotle took up position behind Bridge on the walkway surrounding the top tier of seats. Bridge hated that his bodyguard had to stand most of the night, but his clients wouldn't expect "the help" to mingle with the boss.

Bridge ordered a cheaper single-malt scotch to sip on, asking the waitress to tell the band he was in the building. His first client was Bobby Ardent, the male half of the Ardents duo. They were a brother and sister team, he the guitarist and songwriter, Candace playing the rest of the instruments. Their recordings were veritable walls of sound, ten and twenty instruments laid on top of each other. Candace would play the piano parts live while using her interface jack to control recordings of the other instruments. Bridge didn't like much popular music, relying on his GlobalNet agents to find him obscure bands from Japan and Chechnya. But the Ardents were interesting, and not just because they were clients.

Bobby appeared in minutes, his demeanor the nervous anticipation of Bridge's typical client. Bobby's request was a simple one. He wanted to spy on his sister. Bobby wanted a full tap on his sister's life, from cameras to GlobalNet to chat transcripts, especially her avatar's actions in the GlobalNet. Of course, he would never admit why he wanted such a thing, and Bridge wouldn't force him. Bridge didn't care that Bobby was in love with his sister. That wasn't germane to the business at hand. Bobby wanted something and Bridge knew a guy. Bobby's excuse was that he wanted to make sure she didn't get involved with the wrong guy. Maybe he even believed that. "Bobby! My favorite rock star!" Bridge greeted the musician with an ear-to-ear grin.

"Hey Bridge, you got it?" Bobby's wrinkled face was coated in a thin film of sweat, his black goatee glistening. Bridge was somewhat distracted by the band's video playing on the shoulder of Bobby's jacket. "Is everything set up?"

"My guy is ready. He just needs the word from you to turn on the tap." Bridge handed over a muted email bizchip. Bobby only had to fingerprint himself on the card and an email would be sent to the contact, a hacker who specialized in surveillance for private dicks, lawyers and tonight, pervy brothers.

"And these are undetectable? She won't know it's there?"

"@Rgonot is good. He's the one who caught Shelley Tilton's hubby fucking around on her. Motherfucker never knew what hit him."

Bobby reached an unsteady hand towards the card. "There's just the little matter of my fee," Bridge interrupted.

Bobby pulled out a PDA, a clunky old tech relic. Bobby was a half-Naturalist, rebelling against technology by refusing to get an interface jack, but he wasn't committed enough to the cause to join the Naturalist communes that were springing up in the remote areas of Montana, Idaho and the Dakotas. The most commitment to anything he'd mustered were a few PSA's decrying the despoiling of the environment by multinational corporations like the one that owned his record label. "You're taken care of. Ten grand in five-year."

Bridge smiled and passed over the bizchip. Bobby grabbed it greedily in both hands, planting his thumbprint forcefully on the scanner. "Message sent," replied the card. Bobby dropped it to the table like it had suddenly burst into flames.

"It's done then," he said as much to himself as to Bridge. Bridge just nodded. "You swear you won't breathe a word of this to anybody?"

"Your priest will spill the beans before I will."

"My priest was a son-of-a-bitch."

"Ain't they all?" Bridge quipped with a laugh. The humor escaped Bobby.

"I gotta go get ready. We're on in ten."

"Awesome. For real. Break a leg or something." As Bobby walked away, Aristotle came over, pointing towards the door. Bridge's next client had entered the hall. Bridge put @Rgonot's card in the table's ashtray and activated its self-

41

destruct code, a program that not only caused the card's physical material to break down, but sent a virus through the GlobalNet that erased the message trail from the card. The only evidence of the transaction was now in Bridge's head and Bobby's conscience.

His next client made Bridge frown. It was Sid Tobin, a wannabe DJ with pretensions of pop greatness. Bridge knew this meeting's script by heart, as they had gone through its motions again and again. Sid wanted a GlobalNet publishing deal and he had no scruples about how it was acquired. Sid's problem was that he was a walking stereotype, the kind that turned off A&R guys. The talent acquisition suits didn't want someone already packaged, they wanted something genuine and authentic that they could then sterilize, commoditize and package as the next big thing. Sid was always trying to cash in on the last big thing a week after it had been abandoned.

By the look of his outfit, Sid was on a Japanese anime hip-hop kick, his features accentuated by makeup to make his eyes look bigger with pointy brows, baggy neon glitter pants and a green glowing jacket festooned with brand labels, gold chains and Nipponese thug slogans. Sid walked with an exaggerated swagger, tossing gang signs as greetings. Before the poseur could even sit, Bridge had already cut him off. "Sid, before you get started, no A&R is going to touch you looking like that. What are those, Hammer Pants?"

"No, no, tomo, I got it all worked out, yo! You know a bunch of A&R guys, right?"

"I know a guy," Bridge repeated almost unconsciously.

"Yo, check it, we throw this blackmail scheme on his ass, right? We get some

42

dirt and throw it in the guy's face and then he's gotta give me a pub deal, yo!" Sid's face was a beaming icon of stupidity, the bullheaded desire overriding any sort of common sense. Bridge just shook his head.

"Do you even know how a blackmail scam is run, you mental midget? First, you actually need to have some dirt on your target. I can assume that since you are coming to me, you don't have any such dirt?" Sid shook his head. "So you'd need to hire someone to find some dirt, a hacker or a PI or something. Then, you'd need a go-between, which I suppose you think is going to be me."

Bridge cut off Sid's excited head nodding. "No, it sure as fuck would not be. That violates my most important rule, I don't touch nothing illegal. Not one fucking thing. And finally, you'd need an A&R guy with such a shitty crop of skeletons in his closet that he'd rather risk his job to sign a complete retard like you than let his dirt get out in the open. You ever met an A&R guy? Yeah, I didn't think so. Well, let me enlighten you. They spend their entire professional careers searching for guys they can sign to the shittiest deals possible, stuffing them full of drugs, hookers and booze until the acts don't know their own fucking names. Once that act is all used up and no good to him anymore, Mr. A&R moves on to the next fucking target. He's a predator with less morals than me. Do you really think he's going to give one shit about his dirty laundry getting aired? They are expected to be shitheels, it's in their job description. He's more likely to kill you than sign you. Use your fucking head, you moron. Did you get a manager like I told you to last time?"

"Shit, Bridge, I don't need no fucking manager. All he's gon' do is take fit'een percent to book me here, and I already got booked here."

"That's because your mom is Twiggs' cousin. Get a manager and let him deal

43

with your fucking ideas. Do you really think I'm going to piss off one of the few A&R guys I know in some half-assed blackmail scam? You can't afford the fee on that sort of shit." Sid whined for a few more minutes before being ushered off. It took the physical presence of Aristotle to get Sid moving on.

Once Sid was gone, Bridge exclaimed, "Aristotle, I swear that kid is going to get himself killed one of these days. He's a dumbass at the genetic level."

"The Buddhists say that all suffering is born of desire," Aristotle began. "By that measure, that little muppet has got lifetimes of suffering to burn off." Bridge grinned at the bodyguard.

"I think he'd literally give up a body part to get signed. You ever hear him?" Aristotle nodded, a pained expression marring his features. "I'd rather listen to two rhinos fucking. Check with Stonewall about Kira when I'm not occupied. I really wanna get that shit taken care of." Aristotle nodded and strode off to find the bouncer.

Bridge's night was business as usual. He met with three other clients in two hours, all routine jobs with minimal payouts. They'd keep the lights on and not much else. With each meeting completed without an appearance from Kira, Bridge's nervousness grew. As small-time as he was, Nicky would be all too happy to follow through on his threats. The quicker he could set Nicky up with the hacker, the quicker he could relax. Finally, around midnight, Aristotle came to his table.

"Kira's outside," he said.

"Well tell him to get his ass in here."

"He won't come in."

"What do you mean he won't come in?"

44

"Exactly that. He refuses to go around the front. He's waiting in the alley across the street. He was exceptionally squirrelly."

"Goddamnit, Angie, can you not give me one clean hacker? Shit, I bet he's hopped up on Trip, all paranoid and shit."

"He didn't look to be speeding so much as genuinely nervous."

Bridge sighed. "Fuck it, I'm done here." He slugged back the last vestiges of his drink. "Let's go meet him. You sure this ain't a setup or something?" Aristotle nodded. "Last thing I need is another beatdown." Bridge stalked out with his bodyguard in tow. He waved to Stonewall as he exited, the Mexican waving back jovially. The asshole bouncer was nowhere to be seen. Maybe Twiggs had fired him for being a cunt to the patrons.

Bridge crossed the street quickly, leaving Aristotle at the alley entrance to cover his back. The alley was deserted, nothing but dumpsters, grime and filth to greet him. "I thought you said he was in here?" Aristotle shrugged. Bridge began walking down the alley, avoiding the puddles of dumpster juice and piles of garbage. The alley smelled of fried rice from the Chinese restaurant.

"PSST. Here." Bridge's head snapped up at the strained whisper. It came from the restaurant's kitchen entrance. "Over here!" Bridge walked slowly to the doorway, his body tensing into some semblance of a fighting stance. His one karate class years earlier had not yielded much beyond embarrassment, but he tried to recall something of the defensive techniques he'd been taught. A head peeked out of the doorway, darting quick glances up and down the alley. "Did anybody follow you?"

"Just Aristotle," Bridge replied, indicating the bodyguard at the other end.

"You wanna tell me why I'm standing ankle deep in shit instead of having a civilized conversation surrounded by hotties in the club?"

"I got people after me," Kira said. Bridge finally got a good look at the kid, and kid he was. He might have been eighteen, but he sure didn't look it. Bridge guessed he had not been shaving too long, and not well at that. His upper lip was covered by a thin wisp of a mustache. Kira's dark hair was tousled, in typical hacker fashion. Even his sideburns were messy. Sweat covered the kid's face, a nervous sweat that seemed to soak his shabby clothes.

'Surely Angie didn't send me one of these homeless squatter hackers,' Bridge thought. The clothes Kira wore weren't cheap, just badly maintained. Brand names were all over his slept in attire. Every movement, every nuance of the kid's body language was nervous paranoia, but an examination of his green eyes told Bridge the kid wasn't tripping. "What are they after you for? Who is they?"

"I found something, something I shouldn't have."

"Ok, well that's nothing to me, kid," Bridge replied, raising his hands to fend off whatever bad mojo the kid had acquired. "I just need you to do a couple of jobs for some clients of mine and..."

"No, Bridge man, you gotta see this, it's... you gotta see who it is!"

"Whoa, I don't see nothing. I don't touch nothing. Whatever you got going on, you keep it to your damn self. All I do is hook you up with someone that wants to buy or sell. I'm the Bridge, not the warehouse, dig?"

Kira's agitation spilled over, his hands grabbing Bridge's coat in a death grip. "You have to see it! Please, I gotta get rid of this! I don't want nothing to do with it! You gotta take it off my hands!"

Bridge pushed the hacker away forcefully. Aristotle strode two steps into the alley. "No, I don't. Sell it to Angie, she can find you a buyer." A red light blinded Bridge for a second. Raising his hand to cover his eyes, he saw three pinpricks of red at the end of the alley. His mind processed the image in slow-motion.

Silhouettes, armed. Three armed men coming down the alleyway towards him from the darkness.

"They'll kill me, Bridge, you gotta take this off my hands," were the last words Bridge heard before the shots rang out. He was thrown to the ground by the force of the body hitting him, his vision blurring with pain.

Chapter 5
August 30, 2028
12:02 a.m.

The dead weight of Kira's falling body crushed the wind out of Bridge's lungs. Kira was a skinny stick figure but the force of the shots had thrown his full weight into Bridge. He clattered to the ground gasping for air, flailing to grasp the reality of the situation. Warm blood quickly soaked his hands as he tried to push Kira's body away. His back was soaked through to the skin underneath by the wet pavement. Flitting thoughts jetted through his mind. 'Getting this suit clean is going to be a bitch,' and 'I have to find another hacker for Nicky' and other equally unimportant truisms passed through his mind. As footsteps echoed towards him, panic set in. 'I'm still alive and they're coming to finish me off.'

The pressure on his chest was suddenly removed, replaced by the tramp of a boot heel. One quick stomp on the sternum, then the boot rested on his chest with enough force to push what little air remained in his lungs out again. "Oi, cunt-face, where is it?" Bridge gasped wordlessly. "I'm talking to you, you tosser." The bouncer Paulie stood on top of Bridge firing staccato questions into his face with that thick English accent. Two others dressed in black with cybershade implants were searching Kira's body with all the finesse of rampaging bison. Kira coughed a wad of blood into one of the men's faces and was rewarded with a vicious punch. Kira's breathing became a loud wet gurgling, a sound Bridge had heard before. The hacker didn't have long left.

A hard slap across the face brought Bridge back to the man towering over him. "Look here, Polly. I got no time to fuck about. That little turd over there gave you something, didn't he? Where is it?"

Bridge struggled for breath, but managed a weak, "He didn't give me nothing. I don't even know him."

"We know he was coming to meet you." Kick to the ribs. "If I start breaking bits off you, you think you'd remember better?" Bridge didn't respond and took another kick to the ribs. "I ain't got all night. Convince me I shouldn't put a fucking bullet in your head and go have a pint, or I swear I will fucking murder you, Polly."

Bridge coughed hard, raising a hand to forestall the beating. "Hey, hey, I'm a talker, not a fighter. Let me just catch my breath and we can figure this out. You need something and he has... had it. I know a guy can find things for you. I won't even charge a fee."

Paulie grabbed Bridge's left arm and began to twist, digging his foot into Bridge's chest to maximize the painful leverage. He glanced over to his companions and said, "You lot find anything?" They shook their heads. "Right, well that does you then, don't it? We'll go toss his place after we take care of this cunt." He reached into his coat, retrieving a gigantic pistol from its holster.

A trashcan slammed into his forehead loudly, sending the gun and its owner flying. Bridge rolled over and sucked in precious, stinking air, his face caked with alley mud. At first, the sounds of scuffle barely penetrated the veil of pain, but his head finally cleared enough to comprehend the scene. The two gunmen were being beaten down by a combination of Aristotle's pummeling fists and Stonewall's flying feet. Surprise had given them the edge, and they were taking full advantage of it. Stonewall quickly finished off his opponent with a knee to the bridge of the nose, the metal of Stonewall's cybernetic leg making a sickening crunching sound. Aristotle chose a more direct elbow and fist combination that was equally effective. Bridge spotted Paulie crawling towards his gun, a gash in the forehead pouring blood. Bridge kicked out, catching the cockney enforcer in the ribs. He struggled to his feet, landing another staggered kick into Paulie's midsection. "How you like that, huh!? You like that, bitch? Who are you working for?" Bridge stammered as he continued to dropkick the groaning figure.

"Fuck off," was the only answer given, so Bridge planted another kick to the ribs. Stonewall, having finished his man, walked over and stomped Paulie's gun hand. The resulting shrieks of pain gave Bridge no small amount of satisfaction. Stonewall used the gun to clock Paulie across the back of the skull, rendering him unconscious.

Aristotle put a hand on Bridge's shoulder. "How bad are you hurt?" he asked.

"I'm ok," Bridge replied, though he wasn't. He felt like hell. His ribs were on fire though thankfully not broken, his lungs were bursting with each breath, and he could still feel the impression of a boot on his chest. Paulie knew how to hurt a man. His mouth filled with the coppery saltiness of a bloody lip, and he spat to clear it. "What the hell are you doing wading in there like that? I'm not paying for that."

"It's hard to extract payment from a coffin," was Aristotle's bemused reply. His grin was ear to ear, the sort of smile that could cheer up any situation. "Consider it an advance."

"Well, my cash flow just got perforated." Bridge indicated Kira's prone body. "You kill those guys?"

Stonewall shook his head. "Not yet, amigo, though I'm betting that one don't have long," he said, pointing at the one he'd kneed in the face. The unconscious tough guy's breathing was a raspy burble. Stonewall's tone indicated that theirs would be a temporary reprieve. "This *cabrón* is getting it last. He gets to watch what I'm gonna do to these two. I told Twiggs, I told him there was something not right about that guy. What'd they want?"

"Don't know. Kira was scared shitless, kept talking about me having to take something from him. Then they shot him."

"Maybe he has whatever it is on him," Aristotle said.

The three men looked at each other uneasily. None relished the idea of searching a dead body. "Don't look at me, I don't want whatever it is anyway!" Bridge exclaimed.

"You don't pay me enough," Aristotle replied flatly.

Stonewall deferred as well. "Hey, I gotta take care of these assholes." Bridge resigned himself to the task and bent down to examine the corpse gingerly with a scowl. He touched Kira's shirt with his fingertips, as if the body was on fire. A bloody, wet cough caused Bridge to throw himself back on his hands. Kira moved, rolling over on his side and opening his mouth to release a gigantic gob of blood.

"FUCK! He's still alive." Bridge crawled quickly over to Kira. "Call an ambulance or the cops or something."

"Twiggs wouldn't appreciate the cops on his doorstep."

"We can't just let him die here!"

"Look at him, Bridge. He ain't making it."

Bridge cursed loudly. "Kira, Kira, it's Bridge. Can you hear me?" The hacker nodded his head weakly. "Kira, what were they after?" The punk's lips were moving, weakly attempting to mouth words that were drowned by the blood. Bridge knelt closer until he could finally make it out.

"You... you'll find... out, bro. I... sent it... man, I can't... I can't feel... my legs. I'm... dying, ain't I? Don't... don't let me..." With that, Kira breathed one final wet gurgle and fell silent.

"What? What the fuck does that..." Bridge began, his jaw snapping shut as he realized what the dead hacker meant. Moving his hands to the base of Kira's skull, he searched for the thing he feared he'd find. Pulling back Kira's hair, he saw the kid's interface jack, the silvery metal flush with the skin of the neck. Poking out of the jack was a wireless adapter.

Bridge was familiar with the hardware, though he had rarely used it. Jacking into a crèche or a street term took a wired connection. The wireless adapter allowed the hacker to access the GlobalNet without a jack from anywhere a hot spot existed, which was just about everywhere in the country outside of rural areas. Kira had been connected the whole time, and that meant he could have sent Bridge any kind of digital file in existence. Whatever Kira had been trying to pawn off, he'd probably succeeded. "Fuck. He sent me something."

"What?"

"Don't know and I really don't want to find out. Goddamnit! I do not want to be in whatever this is. That is not my goddamn business. My business is bullshit. You want your shit, you go to the guy I tell you to. That's it. Simple. Don't involve me, just pay me your fucking money, you festering pack of idiots, and leave me the fuck alone. And what does this little bastard do? He gets this all over me!" Bridge indicated the blood on his hands before wiping them off as best he could on Kira's pants. Bridge ceased ranting and stood, buried in thought.

"Stoney, can you deal with this body for me?" Stonewall nodded. "And take these bastards, find out what they were looking for, who they told, who they're working for. Anything you can." The ex-footballer nodded again. "If I'm going to be in this, damnit, I'm not doing it without knowing all the particulars. Do what you gotta do. You won't hear me crying, got it?"

"What do you want me to do, boss?" Aristotle asked with earnest concern.

"Go home. Your bill is already past due." Aristotle started to protest. "If I need you, I know where to find you. But these guys aren't going to be scared off by a big black man, which means you stick around, you'll have to do a lot more of this." The bodyguard looked hurt but agreed. "Help Stoney move these guys out of sight, then get home and stay there."

"What are you going to do?"

"What I do best. Cover my ass." His confident smile was anything but.

Bridge caught a passing cab a few blocks over, took it three blocks in one direction, hopped out and caught another cab going the opposite direction for eight blocks. He got out of the cab at a corner terminal. Called street terms, these kiosks were found every few blocks in LA, offering cheap GlobalNet access, banking, news sheets, driving directions, tourist information and food delivery services. Bridge used an old backup hacker ID to access the GlobalNet and called Angela. He crouched low beside the term, the cord to his interface jack stretched perilously.

Memories of teenage street hacking came flooding back, years of nickel and dime hacks riding the Net while keeping meat vision lookouts for the cops. He constantly searched for pursuit. His paranoia was likely misplaced, since the ID he'd signed in with wasn't tied to the Bridge name at all, but he hadn't survived this long by being careless. And if the Bridge ID was already hot as he suspected, this one would be burned once he was done.

Angela returned the request with a physical presence, projecting her avatar onto his vision. She appeared as a wispy ghost, beautiful blonde angel with demon horns and gossamer wings floating in mid-air on the street in front of him. "What's wrong?"

"Why do you think something's wrong?" Bridge put on his best fake smile.

"Because you haven't used B#rTman in ages, which means you don't want somebody following your trail. Now what's wrong?"

"Kira's dead." The ghost chewed on that for a moment. "He was trying to give me something, said somebody was after him for it. Bunch of guys shot him and tried to shake me down for something Kira had. We took care of the guys..."

"Who's we?"

"Never mind that. I'm alive, he's dead and I need to know what he was working."

"Nothing major." Bridge frowned doubtfully. "No really, nothing big. We were messing with some pedofarms, but nothing that would get him killed. These guys, they look like organized muscle?"

"They weren't cheap. Good clothes, cybershades, laser-sights, big guns and the like."

"As far as I know, nobody he was working on was connected like that. Where's the body?"

"It's being taken care of."

"So I shouldn't tell his mom, then?"

"Not unless you want it tied to you." She shook her head ruefully. "I think he sent me some kind of package before he died, probably whatever he was trying to get rid of. I can't go to my place, in case those assholes reported back to their bosses."

"Here it comes."

"Look, I just need a place to crash for a few days, 'til I can get this sorted."

"Don't you have any friends?"

"When did I ever have friends I could impose on like you?"

She sighed angrily. "Few days tops. And I better not get any heat over this, or it's your ass."

"The first sign of heat, I'm gone. I promise."

Her scowl was an accusation. "Save it. I know what your promise is worth. You owe me. AGAIN."

He cut off the connection, muttering under his breath, "More than you know." With creeping dread, he switched Net ID's, accessing the Bridge mailbox. Buried among the assorted spam offers and regular mail was a message from Kira, bloated with an attachment. Kira must have been good to float an attachment past Bridge's filtering system. He sighed and jacked out without reading the message. He'd wait to get to Angela's, where he could open it from the detached safety of a clean room. He called another cab, beginning an hour merry-go-round of cab switching, route retracing and obfuscation. By the time he reached Angela's place exhausted and bruised, it was almost two a.m.

Chapter 6
August 30, 2028
2:07 a.m.

"You look like shit, Artie. Is that blood?"

The crackling static of Angela's disembodied voice was a painfully welcome reminder of past days. Bridge stood at her door, disheveled and battered, staring up at the camera above the door, which was no doubt displaying his sorry self on a window in Angela's crèche. "You should see the other guys," Bridge quipped. "They look like a million bucks."

"You always were a cream puff. Door's open." Bridge heard the latch on the door click and pushed through quickly, keeping an eye out until the door closed. The latches and bolts slammed back into place automatically as soon as the door was shut. Even so, Bridge flattened against the wall and edged up to the front window overlooking the apartment complex's deserted pool. A pricey place like this likely attracted a 9-5 corporate clientele that would rarely be up this late on a work night. Angela had done well since ditching him.

"Nice place you got here."

"Business is good." Angela's voice came from all around Bridge. Her wispy body materialized out of thin air, the perfect holographic representation of one of her avatars. Her real body looked almost nothing like this. Seven feet tall, bleached-bone white skin and jet hair flowing to her knees, with fingernails just short of being claws, this was Santhariya, the queen of the night realm, Orphonus.

Bridge raised an eyebrow. "Very good, apparently. Those holo projectors aren't cheap."

"Kim got me a got a good deal on them. This guy wanted me to steal some prototype designs, so he gave me the old models for like half price. I can't resist a bargain."

"Especially when it involves a run, right?" Her avatar nodded quickly, that cute mischievous smile Bridge was so familiar with in the flesh transferred to this apparition perfectly.

"So where are you?"

"Back in the bedroom," she said, indicating a room past the open kitchen. The apartment itself was so sparsely furnished Bridge could barely tell it was occupied. An expensive, barely creased couch was a deserted island in the middle of a desolate living area, positioned directly in front of the wall screen. The kitchen was the only area that appeared used, and badly used at that. Dishes caked with crusted food piled in the sink, used cardboard food containers left torn on the filthy counters. He'd seen this type of thing in so many different hackers' homes that it might have been its own interior design style for the cyberpunk set. Most of the dedicated hackers spent more time in the crèche than the flesh, and as a result, they needed little furniture and cared even less for homemaking.

"Can I at least talk to your face?"

A tiny frown creased her lips. "I'm hardly decent," she joked. "I'm deep in, Bridge, I don't have time to swab off and be a hostess. There's food in the fridge if you want, the couch is as good as a bed. Now what the fuck happened to my hacker?"

"I told you, something he found got him killed. You said he was hitting pedofarms. What did you do?" His accusatory tone sounded harsher than he intended.

She put her balled fists on her hips, the first signs of her obstinate attitude emerging. "I didn't do anything. I sent a few guys on some fun runs, a little harmless griefing." Bridge's frown caused Angela to point her finger accusingly. "You used to enjoy that."

"That's the kind of shit got Margie killed."

"Margie got sloppy. You don't shack up with the guys you're griefing. Look, all we did was put some recorders on these ageplay sims. Find a few pervs paying for cybersex with underage avatars, record their escapades then send it to their wives. We didn't even ask for blackmail money. We just wanted to fuck with them."

Bridge sighed and rubbed his forehead. "And if one of those guys happened to be connected, he'd damn sure not hesitate to pop a cap in Kira's ass." Bridge's mind raced despite his exhaustion. "Kira sent me an attachment, but I'm not looking at it without a clean room and a backup ID. Can I borrow a crèche?"

Angela frowned. "I have an old one, but it's slow." To Angela, if it wasn't built last week with firmware upgraded last night, it was a decrepit dinosaur slogging through a primordial swamp.

"How old?"

"May? April? I kind of lost track after I got this one." Bridge was impressed, and a little bit proud. Angela really was doing quite well, as none of the stuff she was purchasing was cheap. Holo projectors and a new crèche every season cost major cash. Of course, never leaving the apartment meant she didn't need a car, and the crèche's nutrient drips meant she probably ate one meal a day if she was lucky. A hacker's life was a series of tradeoffs normal schlubs never made. "It should do for watching a run replay. Just don't use an ID that could connect with me."

"Got it. Now, where is this thing?"

"Bedroom. Come on back." Bridge shuffled hesitantly down the apartment's central hallway. Angela wouldn't come out of the crèche to greet him, and he was certainly unsure he wanted to walk around in the room while she lay unmoving in the little pillbox. Even proximity to her avatar was enough to bring back painful memories.

The bedroom was as sparsely furnished as the rest of the place, and just as messy. A few takeout boxes lay on the floor. The bed was simply a mattress thrown haphazardly on the floor, sheets tousled and unkempt. The low hum of the crèche's cooling unit filled the room. The shiny black surface of the coffin-like device was decorated with lines of neon green LED strips, a sign of heavy modification both on the exterior and the interior. "It's that one over there," Angela said, pointing in the corner at a dusty plain crèche. Bridge wiped his finger through the thick layer of dust. "The maid is off this year," Angela joked.

"Has it got the basics? Security package, mail, etc.?"

"Do I ever work with the basics? Hell, no, that thing has custom warez. I think the defense package even has your codebase. I abandoned that tack when Freeman put out his Plat Series." Bridge was postponing the jack in, running his hands over the console at the base of the device. He powered the crèche on, looking at the lights for entirely too long in an effort to forestall the inevitable.

He didn't want to jack in. He'd sworn off the whole life. Like a recovering alcoholic, he marked each day without a jack in as an accomplishment. It was an exciting life, cutting through databank security and pilfering whatever he could, battling live Net security agents in some liquid mercury duel with programs he built from the ground up. The full-on speed of a crèche run was so different from just jacking into the front of the crèche. If a regular jack run was a sprint, a crèche run was a drag race, an intense compression of time and speed and data folded into every erg of consciousness. That kind of intensity couldn't be easily put down, and once Bridge had removed himself from those runs, he'd felt their absence every goddamn day.

"What are you waiting for? Get naked!"

Bridge scowled back at the avatar and began to strip off his clothes. "It might help a bit if I didn't have the Virtual Voyeur watching me."

"It's nothing I haven't seen before." That didn't help Bridge's nervousness much.

"It's cold in here," Bridge joked as he dropped his shorts, turning quickly to lift the lid.

"That's what you always say." The bubbling, mischievous giggle brought a flush to Bridge's cheek, and a pang of nostalgia to his heart. The crèche's soft plastic interior was chilly, its flesh-like embrace surrounding him with a womblike familiarity. Fitting the urine catch caused more jokes at his genitals' expense. The nutrient drip into his arm was a bit more difficult than usual. It had been a while since he'd tapped that vein, and he'd had the easy-access cap removed. He closed the lid firmly, cutting off the teasing and encasing him in the silence of a tomb. The breathing apparatus covered his face and eyes as the saline solution flooded the chamber, a brief cold snap before the internal warmers kicked in. Within seconds, the interior of the coffin was a dimly-lit liquid paradise, his body covered with a slick fluid as his senses were one by one deprived of input. The jack began to do its magic, booting up the interface sequence. The last physical sound he heard was the beep signifying the bootup sequence's completion.

And then he flew headlong into a wall of white, a bright onrush of euphoric experience that seemed to permeate every cell in his body. That one instant of elation was what the real hacker lived for, that sensation of flying warp speed into the great overmind, the digitization of consciousness that signaled immersion in the waters of the collected knowledge of humankind. The feeling was as close to being God as Bridge had ever thought his frail human mind could experience. The process was instantaneous, but it stretched the mind so hard that time elongated, eternity compressed into a single intense moment.

His NetBody rezzed into the crèche's foyer, and the sensation was gone like gossamer on the wind. It was replaced with the liquid motion of his NetBody, a shiny slick humanoid-shape with the properties of liquid mercury. The programs he chose to carry with him would reshape the NetBody in various ways, some offensive, others defensive.

Accessing one of his backup ID's had equipped the NetBody with his favored weapon, a dual-edged spear and his personal defense, a buckler-shaped shield. He tested the programs, swinging the weapons and running through a few Net-fu forms, a kind of martial arts based fighting style that hackers had adapted to Net combat. He hoped not to see any Net combat, but his paranoia about the situation caused him to prepare. Checking a few of his data gathering and analysis programs, he proceeded out of the foyer. The inky black space between data nodes was an infinite expanse of beauty, an empty void filled with the twinkling stars of billions of data nodes, web sites, chat rooms and virtual worlds.

His first steps were to hide the trail of his NetBody, sending the packets bouncing around the world in the blink of an eye, leaving traces of its passing in hundreds of random locations around the globe. Someone trying to backtrack to his physical location would need to unravel the mass of dead-end IP addresses and false trails before finding his vulnerable body, and their detection would alarm Bridge in enough time to allow him to jack out safely. Once assured his trail was sufficiently obscured, he rented a "clean room," an off-the-shelf data location on the GlobalNet that contained no previous data, no programs, and only one entrance. He could control data access to the room, making sure that whatever he brought in could not leave without his knowledge, as well as ensuring that someone attempting to find him would have only one avenue of attack.

He marveled at the speed with which he worked. Not for the first time did Bridge consider dropping his work in the meat world and going back to hacking. The rush of adrenaline was real, an ever present euphoric call.

Putting aside the desire to backslide into his previous life, he sent out a request, a backdoor call to his Bridge ID's mailbox. The request grabbed the email from Kira and sent it flying around the Net, obscuring it's destination as surely as he'd done for his NetBody. The message appeared in the clean room as a blinking envelope icon, vaguely three-dimensional floating in mid-air. Bridge sighed and opened the message.

The body of the message was brief. Kira had sent it with his last breath, and all it contained was the plaintive cry, "Watch me!" Bridge felt like kicking Kira square in the junk. The attachment was large. Bridge extracted it from the message, analyzing it with one of his data-sniffing programs. It was dense, likely a room recorder. Much like a hidden camera placed in a physical room, a room recorder captured all the data of a NetRoom, creating an exact duplicate of the room, its occupants and their actions that could be experienced again. Viewing the recorder's contents in the proper program would give the viewer a voyeuristic experience from any angle but without the ability to alter the proceedings. The viewer could even take the place of one of the participants, hitching a passive ride in the participant's mind, feeling every sensation the person felt during that time. Such recordings were popular on the Net, most being pornographic.

Bridge dropped himself into the recording as a spectator. The room was not surprising, given the nature of Kira's targets. Bridge could only describe it as a stereotypical little girl's room, posters of teenage heartthrobs on the wall, stuffed animals neatly placed in a parade around the walls. The single bed was festooned in pink and puffy lace, the walls even painted a girly pink. Fake sunlight flickered through a window, and one door led out of the room. The room's occupant rezzed in, and Bridge's gorge rose.

A little girl, no older than twelve years had appeared, sitting on the bed, chewing gum and blowing bubbles while twisting her finger through her pigtails. It was a painfully stereotypical scene. Bridge immediately accessed information on the avatar. According to the room, she was actually a twenty-six year old virtual escort who worked out of Colorado. Despite knowing that this underage avatar was a consenting adult, he still felt queasy about what he knew was coming next. The door to the bedroom opened slowly, an adult male sneaking into the room like a thief.

The accompanying rape fantasy was by the numbers, the adult forcing himself upon the child in a disgusting display of oedipal dominance. Even though it was an act that didn't involve an actual child, it still made Bridge's stomach turn. This kind of ageplay sold well on the porn market. It wasn't illegal, though most courts frowned on virtual escort services as well as the disgusting implications of virtual child rape. It would be extremely damaging for anyone caught partaking, causing divorces and firings at the least. Bridge felt no remorse for closet pedophiles like this one whose life would be upended by the revelation of such predilections.

As he watched the scene, the doughy face of the man started to seem familiar. Had he not been so disgusted by the acts portrayed, Bridge would have recognized the man immediately. The avatar was almost the spitting image of Mayor Oliver Sunderland. That in itself was odd. Participants in these types of rooms typically chose attractive avatars, and Sunderland was hardly that. He was a pudgy man in his early 50's, the kind of nondescript pudding of a man that would be no one's ideal fantasy. Bridge began to get a sinking feeling and reluctantly accessed the identity of the man. All he could do was shake his head in disbelief. The person running the avatar was by all accounts exactly who he appeared to be. It was the Mayor of Los Angeles, Oliver Sunderland.

Bridge cursed a blue streak. This was exactly the kind of thing that could get a hacker killed. Powerful men with embarrassing secrets guarded those secrets with the violence of a cornered tiger. Their handlers would not hesitate to disappear someone as insignificant as Kira or Bridge to keep this kind of thing quiet.

Bridge's first thought was to delete any trace of the file, but he hesitated. Paulie and his employers likely already knew about Bridge. They had tracked Kira to the Arsenal, going so far as to install Paulie in a job there to make sure the hacker was caught and killed. Deleting the file would remove what little leverage Bridge had. And after what Twiggs' guys were likely doing to Paulie and his flunkies this very minute, Paulie's employer wasn't likely to balk at killing Bridge even if the file was gone. No, Bridge was stuck with it.

So he had to find a way to use it.

He could blackmail Sunderland. But like he'd told Sid earlier, a blackmail scam was the last thing he wanted to get involved with, especially if he was the blackmailer. Blackmail money was hard as hell to collect. But Sunderland's place in the public eye left him vulnerable. He had enemies.

As Bridge pondered his next move, he failed to notice that the entrance to the clean room had opened. If he'd been in his physical body, the sensation that warned him of the coming attack would have been an itching at the base of his skull. Luckily, he had the room wired to alert him of any entrances, authorized or not. Bridge kept still, presenting as easy a target as he could without leaving himself completely vulnerable. A moment before the first blow struck, Bridge twisted his NetBody to place the shield arm between him and the attacker. Losing the arm was a screaming white light of pain in his brain, the limb dissolving from the forearm down in a mist of mercury droplets.

Chapter 7
August 30, 2028
3:34 a.m.

The loss of a Netlimb was a queer sensation, a kind of panicked tickling as the brain strained to maintain its binary illusion that there actually was a limb where a limb no longer existed. The reptile brain wanted the body to feel the pain, to feel the warning that pain symbolized, yet the logical brain refused to allow the NetBody to lose its cohesion. Bridge knew he was in for a real bruise on the arm when he left the crèche, as his physical limb thrashed around wildly to reassure itself of its reality. For now, his immediate thoughts were on reforming the arm into a shield and setting himself into a defensive posture.

The attack had come swiftly, and Bridge's practically antiquated software package had given him too little warning. He quickly sized up his opponent while dodging the second strike, a vicious spear stabbing inches from his side as his body flowed around the thrust.

The attacker was much faster than Bridge could hope to be with this setup. His silvery body held a barely humanoid shape with animal-like feet. Hooves, as a matter of fact, the guy had hooves. His entire lower half reminded Bridge of a shaven billy goat, as if the body was modeled after a satyr. The right arm was an elongated axe, the left a spear. At the top of his smooth head was a gigantic pair of horns, dripping with a virus-injector's poisonous code. Bridge was in serious trouble. His opponent was built for all-out attack, and Bridge's defenses were slow and outdated. He dodged another slice of the axe and tried to circle around towards the exit but found his path blocked by the spear.

Bridge aimed a quick sword thrust at the attacker's midsection, but found it easily parried by the axe. Only a quick twist of the shield protected his chest from another spear thrust. Bridge retreated a moment. The attacker had the advantage of reach, and despite being on Bridge's turf, the room afforded no particular advantage to either combatant. Any attempt to make it to the door would likely end with Bridge skewered and gored. Once caught, those horns would likely deliver a virus that would flatline his real heartbeat.

"Who are you?" Bridge asked, breaking arena protocol. No one talked in arena battles, at least not until they had won. The smack talk would begin in earnest afterwards, of course, provided both parties survived. But it was bad form to speak during combat.

The voice that replied was heavily synthesized, a devil-reverb effect applied for maximum intimidation. "I am your DOOM!" Bridge really did not like this guy now.

"What a douchebag," he said. The insult drew the attacker in like a lightning bolt, the spear diving straight for Bridge's center. Bridge launched one of his better trick programs, the meat trap. His body opened at the point of attack, the deadly spear passing harmlessly through the hoop that Bridge's chest had become. Bridge then closed the loop, chopping the spear arm off at the wrist. A follow up sword swipe was parried easily by the intruder's axe, but Bridge had made some needed breathing room.

He quickly packaged the recording into a peer-to-peer rocket, breaking the bits up into unrelated junk data and encapsulating them in a sort of cluster bomb. Firing the rocket off sent the packets hurtling through the exit, where the rocket would "explode," scattering the junk data all over the GlobalNet. The data would latch itself onto bigger data packets like barnacles and ride those packets forever until Bridge sent out the recall order. The packets would then return and condense into something usable, provided Bridge survived the fight. Now Bridge had to hope he had time to enact the other part of his desperation gambit.

Bridge began dancing about the room, twisting and turning like a snake, flying from corner to corner dodging attacks, buying time for himself and the rocket. The walls shook with the axe swings that just barely missed contact with Bridge, the room beginning to lose cohesion as bits were chipped off. The rocket seemed to be moving in slow motion. Just as it reached the exit, the door opened to allow another player's entrance. The new entrant dodged the rocket with ease despite being surprised.

Bridge initiated his jack out sequence as the dancing continued. Had he any other choice, he'd have taken it, but the attacker had him in a corner. Bridge would jack out the hard way, without returning his consciousness along the path he'd taken to get there. It would be akin to pulling the plug on his crèche, a jarring return to physical consciousness that was painful in the extreme. Rather than the gradual return to his body of a normal shutdown procedure, this would be a shocking snap, and he would suffer for it. Headaches, nosebleeds and the choking claustrophobia of the coffin were the most common side effects.

The sudden jack out still took nanoseconds, and he was defenseless the whole time. He could see the killing axe blow swinging toward his head. He flinched from the blow that never came. The axe arm was dissolved with the swing of a scythe blade, the droplets of NetBody floating weightlessly away. Bridge's last visible image was of Angela's liche-like avatar swinging her impossibly large scythe through the attacker's neck with ruthless efficiency.

And then he was alive, the crèche's inky black interior suffocating him. He flailed inside the pill-shaped coffin, the saline solution splashing, his muscles twitching in uncontrollable spasms of solidity. His mind was a bubbling cauldron of fear, thoughts sizzling inside his skull, burning his light-starved eyes. He couldn't move, couldn't run though his every nerve was on fire, his cells raging with the desire for motion, for the surety of existence in activity.

Finally, decades later, the crèche's latch opened and he threw back the lid, flopping out onto the floor like a fish out of water. His muscles still weren't working right. The arm he'd lost in the GlobalNet was there, but he could see bruising up and down the forearm area, and he couldn't force it to move no matter how hard he concentrated. His entire body refused mental commands, the jack out seizure in full control.

He wasn't sure how long he lay like that, twitching and flopping uncontrollably until the tremors finally slowed, crashing then ebbing like the waves at high tide. He was still twitching slightly when Angela's holographic form appeared above him.

"You gonna die on me?" she asked with a tinge of real concern.

He swallowed hard and tried to reply, but nothing would come out but a raspy exhalation.

"Take it slow. You haven't done this for a while, remember." He nodded.

His voice returned weakly. "How did you find me?"

"It's my crèche. I can track it anywhere. Plus your trail wasn't exactly hidden well enough. That's some old shit you were running."

"I haven't kept up."

"No, you haven't. I figured you'd get in some shit, so I followed you. Just in time, too." She held something in her ghostly hand, which he finally realized was a head. "Do you know Ub3r||M3^^?" He shook his head. "He knew you, apparently. Looks like whatever you got yourself into was worth hiring a hitter."

"He's a hitter?"

"According to his creds he was. Not a very good one, obviously. He didn't even bother credcrashing you. Sloppy dip shit. He probably did tag your accounts, though, so I wouldn't use your creds if I was you."

"I haven't used cred since I quit hacking. It's why I only take five-year." His strength had returned enough to sit up, though his left arm was going to be sore for days. "Crashers don't fuck with the cash vendors. Those boys will fuck back."

"So what did you find that's important enough to put a hit out on you?"

Bridge relayed the sorted story of Kira's big find. Angela seemed genuinely angry that the Mayor of the city was a closet pedophile and even more so that his proclivities had gotten her hacker killed. By the time he'd finished, her jaw was clenched so tight he could imagine her cheek muscles twitching with the exertion. Her eyes were flaming red coals.

"What are you going to do to nail this son-of-a-bitch?"

Bridge hadn't gotten that far. Nailing Sunderland, while certainly a tempting prospect, wasn't his first thought. "I'm less concerned about nailing him than I am about keeping his bastards from bumping me off."

"You're going to let him get away with this?"

"Get away with what? The guy playing his little girlfriend is a 26-year old grad student in Colorado. He hasn't broken any laws, and even if he had, he's the goddamn mayor. He has Chronosoft on his side. You don't think they could cover this shit up?"

"So what, he just walks? He killed my hacker."

"And that's fucked me up just as much as you. I got clients ready to beat me blue again if I don't get them somebody. So I either gotta find another guy or pay money I don't have to keep them from breaking my legs or worse." Bridge's mind was in overdrive now that his body was more or less normalized. He was examining angles and profit margins, analyzing risks and thinking on his feet. "But there is a way I can get rid of this thing and recoup my losses on the deal."

"Your losses? What about my losses?"

"You'll get your cut too. If I take the footage to Sunderland's folks, they'll probably just kill me to cover it up. Since he didn't technically do anything illegal, I can't go to the cops with it, and they don't pay for shit anyway." He looked up at Angela's avatar with a kind of puppy dog helplessness. "You know, you could sell it for me."

"Don't even get me more involved in this than I already am."

"Come on, Angie, do me a solid. You're the best broker I know."

She cut him off with a dismissive wave of her ghostly hand. "Save the sweet talking for your clients. I know you too well."

"No sweet talk. Seriously, you could sell this shit before I wake up in the morning."

"And we'd both be dead by the time we were done with breakfast. No deal, slick. I'm not ending up like Kira."

Bridge set his jaw with the grim realization of his predicament. "Well, there is one person who'd give his left nut for something like this, especially right now."

"Who?"

Bridge shook his head, shutting off his audible rambling. "If you ain't selling it, better you don't know. The less people involved, the less targets they have. You sure you don't mind me crashing here for a few?"

"Just crashing. No business in the house."

"I just need a place nobody knows about for a few days, then I'll be out of your hair and I can compensate you some for Kira. How's twenty percent sound?"

She thought hard for a moment before replying, "Not as good as thirty."

"Twenty-five."

"Done."

Bridge wobbled to his feet. "Right then, I'm going to shower this shit off and crash on the couch. I better get moving early tomorrow. Don't want to sit still too long." The shower did wonders to loosen the stiffness in his muscles from the emergency jack out seizure, but his head was splitting. Popping an Aceto™ tab, he flopped on the couch, trying to sleep through the dancing fireflies of pain behind his eyes. The plan raced through his head threatening sleeplessness, but his body gave up consciousness before he had a chance to toss.

Chapter 8
August 30, 2028
9:13 a.m.

Bridge woke early, fixed a light breakfast and headed out without a word to Angela. She never showed, in holograph or in person, so he assumed she'd either passed out or was still running deep. He was glad not to have to talk to her again. If she wasn't going to help him get rid of the recording, best she wasn't involved in what he had planned next.

Since this Sunderland data had already almost gotten him killed and given him his second beatdown in twenty-four hours, he was committed to ridding himself of this data in the safest way possible. He wasn't yet desperate enough to try to blackmail Sunderland. Though the mayor had the means, he'd be just as likely to kill everyone involved as pay blackmail money. If Paulie was in Sunderland's employ as Bridge suspected, odds were Sunderland would err on the side of violence.

Without using a go-between, one Bridge could hardly afford to find or pay on such short notice, Bridge was entirely too exposed for blackmail.

Sunderland had enemies, though. He had one big enemy in particular, one who'd welcome the kind of dirty laundry this recording represented. With the election only two days away, the value of the information was reaching its apex, so time was short. After the election, the information would only be valuable if Sunderland retained his post and even then, its value would sink like a stone with each passing day. But while the voters were still being inundated with the candidate's message, one person in particular would pay a king's ransom for this kind of bombshell.

That was why Bridge stood across the street from the campaign headquarters of Sunderland's opponent, Arturo Soto. In keeping with Soto's anti-corporate political stance, it was a modest location, a strip mall space leased out and transformed into a buzzing hive of activity. Bridge, being a paranoid fucker, had to marvel at the lax security of the building.

The entire front of the space was clear glass windows from knee height to ceiling, and most areas were clearly visible from his vantage point. One area was clearly designated for the net roots activity, a bank of hastily constructed cubicles barely sheltering a squad of cyber operators posting videos, testimonials, advertisements, rumors, news stories and other such "net roots" information. Most other workers were busily making phone calls or gathering fliers and there was a constant stream of volunteers flowing through the door.

Bridge crossed the street warily. He'd managed to get a new suit to replace the blood-covered one he wore the previous night, ditching the horrible t-shirt and jeans combination Angela had foisted on him from spare clothes she had in her closet. He didn't ask whose clothes they had been. He strode confidently into the front door, flashing the receptionist his most charming, nano-enhanced smile.

The cute blonde behind the desk responded with a dutiful friendliness, but her eyes gave Bridge that little something extra. Bridge was by no means a handsome man. His black hair was slicked back, exposing a burgeoning widow's peak. His nose was perhaps a tad too big and angular, while his face was a bit too doughy from years of stewing motionless in a vat of saline. The five o-clock shadow he sported didn't hurt his appeal. But Bridge had discovered that thing that made him imminently more attractive than his looks. He walked with the confidence of someone who knows how to get what he wants. It didn't hurt that his attitude towards the entirety of humanity was one of loathful indifference.

He showed no sign of caring whether a woman found him attractive or not, and Bridge could only conclude that woman viewed that as a challenge. So it was with the receptionist, Carly.

Bridge made a vain attempt to see Soto himself,

knowing full well that no campaign manager lets just any jagoff get close to the candidate without a thorough vetting. It was a good thing Bridge actually wanted to see the campaign manager. Bridge pretended to settle for this meeting with feigned disappointment. Candidates don't lay their own hands on their opponent's dirty laundry. That's why they hire campaign managers.

Carly ushered Bridge through to the manager's office within minutes. Along the way, she slipped him a note. Bridge knew it contained the woman's phone and NetID, but he feigned surprise for the purpose of the pantomime they were performing. A final wry smile saw Carly out the door.

"Good morning," was the all-business greeting Bridge got from the campaign manager, Barbara Losman. Losman was a young-looking mid-40's, long straight golden brown hair framing an imperfect face that smiled a little too disingenuously. Long smile lines stretched around her perfectly lined lips, her eyes just a bit too wide as if incredulous at the world around her. But underneath that expression, Bridge could sense the most cunning sort of cynicism, a calculating coldness that parsed every fragment of dialogue for the slightest advantage. This was a dangerous woman. "How may I help you, Mister... I'm sorry, I didn't catch your name."

Bridge sat down across from her smoothly. "That's because I didn't give it."

Losman rolled along without batting an eyelash. "Well, I'm Barbara Losman, and it's a pleasure to meet one of the voters. Were you interested in volunteering for the campaign? We're a bit overstaffed, if that's the case, but I'm sure we could find something for you to do."

"I'm here to help you put this election in the bank."

Losman's eyebrow rose almost imperceptibly. She was cautiously intrigued. "That's certainly good news. Are you sure I can't offer you anything? Coffee? Tea? Fresca?" She said the last bit as she shuffled papers on her desk. She attempted to make the movement seem absentminded, but he could tell she was angling to push the security button she likely had under her desk.

"I'm not just some crazy off the street, so you can take your finger off that button," he said with a relaxed smile. One solitary bead of sweat rolled down his left armpit, the tension in the room becoming palpable.

Losman smiled the grin of a predator pleased to finally meet a canny opponent. "Fair enough," she said, raising her hands above the desk before leaning back in her chair. "Since I don't know you, explain to me how you intend to help my candidate win the election."

"Your opponent is about as dirty as they come," Bridge began.

Losman feigned a sarcastic surprise. "No, you don't say! Was it the fact that he was appointed into his position by corporate fiat or the fact that he's done nothing for this city other than bulldoze neighborhoods since he got into office? You could ask any ten people out on the street and nine of them would say he was dirty. You could put a patron saint into his position and at least six would still think he was dirty."

"What if I told you I was in possession of information proving your opponent was engaged in ethically questionable activities that would make all ten of those people throw up?"

The wall came up. Losman's features hardened into an inscrutable blank stare. "I would say that you should be talking to the press. They love a good sex scandal. My candidate isn't interested, no matter what the price."

Bridge was taken aback. He hadn't even mentioned sex or money, but it appeared the negotiations had started without him. "What I have will make sure Sunderland gets fewer votes than drunken Mickey Mouse write-ins. All I need..."

And just like that, the negotiation was over. "You don't understand, so let me make it perfectly clear. My candidate is in no way interested in your seedy scandals. Maybe you haven't checked the polls lately. Soto is ahead amongst just about every demo that matters."

"I do understand that he's both ahead and behind by statistical nothings depending on whose poll you believe. Two days 'til the election and it could go either way. I'm offering you a slam dunk."

"You're offering me the chance to drive this campaign right in the gutter. My client has no interest in those kinds of dirty politics-as-usual."

Bridge couldn't prevent a hint of anger creeping into his voice. "Come on, lady, we both know politics is about as clean as a fucking cesspool, especially in this city. And we both know your client has as much blood on his hands from the riots as any Chronosoft executive. Soto ain't no Richard the Lionhearted, no matter what you're trying to peddle on those commercials of yours."

"Richard the Lionhearted? You're going to go crusaders on me? That's very educated of you."

"I read history, I been to college. That's a good one, eh?"

She smiled a smile so disingenuous it gave the truth whiplash. "Yes, quite impressive." And then she was done playing games. "This meeting is over." Her eyes were simmering coals, and Bridge knew he was wasting his time. "Will you leave quietly, or should I indulge myself and let my security curbstomp you out the door?"

"I'll show myself out," Bridge said coldly, standing and straightening his lapels. He gave her a sarcastic head bow and walked out, barely able to contain his anger. He waited until he'd crossed the street and made it around the corner before letting out a torrent of inventive curses. He began to walk aimlessly, not thinking about a destination, just trying to sort out the puzzle before him.

Soto's people weren't interested in dirt, but that just didn't compute. Politicians spoke ad nauseum about their desire to run clean campaigns, their firm belief in a return to honorable politics as if such a thing had ever existed. But invariably, all political races turned into sleazy, mud-slinging games of one-upmanship. The presidential election of 2020, the first Bridge had voted in, had taught him the scant lessons he knew of politics, and he'd mostly sworn off voting after that bitter experience.

It was beyond Bridge's conception that a politician wouldn't take any opportunity to smear his opponent, especially if done in such a way as to make it appear the smear-er had nothing to do with the smearing. Losman had refused to even consider the option. While both she and the candidate may claim it was because

Soto was some crusading savior, Bridge wasn't buying it. Furthermore, Bridge had never mentioned what exactly it was that Sunderland was involved in, yet Losman had immediately hit upon a sex scandal. That seemed a little too spot on to be a coincidence.

Bridge looked up to find himself in front of a waiting cab. Without even consciously considering it, Bridge had decided on his next course of action. He needed to see Tom Williams.

A quick call to Tom led Bridge to the Press Room, a tiny bar and grill just outside of the downtown area where most of the news broadcasts located their LA bureaus. The Press Room was such a prototypical LA establishment, a darkened private restaurant built in the 1970's. The original décor still insulted the eye with its vomit brown plush carpet, dark faux brick and copious red stained glass. It was the kind of place anyone could walk into, from movie stars to regular schlubs, and the patrons would pay no special attention to anyone, making it the perfect anonymous meeting point for reporters and their sources. Or, in the case of Bridge and Tom Williams, the perfect meeting place for client and provider.

Tom was the kind of man who stood out anywhere he went, a ruggedly beautiful man with perfect blonde hair, teeth and physique. His square jaw was prototypically Midwestern, and his voice had the gravitas to carry a broadcast all on his own for hours. His career had been practically meteoric, from local field man to local anchor to the face of the Chronosoft owned National News Network in 15 years. Luckily for Bridge, in the Press Room, Tom was just the good-looking guy in the corner booth with the slick talker. Tom had needed a source for floating card games, the kind of games no one admitted to running or participating in. Tom had a helluva gambling problem when he was losing, and he'd been close to having that problem exposed when Bridge had taken care of him. Bridge knew a guy.

Bridge's stomach started grumbling as soon as he sat down, so he ordered lunch, while Tom just had coffee. "Like I need anymore caffeine in my day," Tom grumbled to no one in particular. He crossed his hands in front of his chest and gave Bridge a stern look. "So why the fuck did you feel it necessary to call me out at work? I thought you relied on the utmost discretion."

"Under normal circumstances, you'd never hear from me unless you sought me out." Bridge was paddling against a very tough upstream. "This is not a normal day. I've got something big."

"How big?"

"Like break open an election big."

Williams' eyebrow shot straight up, and he seemed to be chewing on the thought. "Elections? Since when did you get involved in politics?"

"Something kind of fell into my lap. Believe me, it's nothing I'd touch otherwise. Would you be interested and more importantly, would that interest be worth anything?"

"That all depends. What election are we talking about?"

"THE election, my friend. Two days from now, the mayor of Los Angeles against the upstart neighborhood crusader. I've got some dirt that is guaranteed to swing this thing..." Bridge paused as the waitress brought the drinks to the table. When she'd left, he continued, "I'm serious, this is national breaking oh my god everyone switch the channel big."

Tom ripped open a packet of sweetener, dumping it unceremoniously into his coffee. He stirred in silent thought, finally lifting the cup and wincing at the heat. Replacing the cup on the table, he shot Bridge down. "I can't touch it."

"What do you mean you can't touch it?"

"I mean I can't touch it. Editorial directive, coming from the very top. No one, and I mean no one, breaks any kind of scandal on this thing first. Me, the guys at CNN, the local guys, nobody can touch any kind of dirt on this election until someone else breaks it first."

"I thought you guys lived to break stories like this, like it was a divine calling." Bridge asked with confused irritation.

Tom chuckled. "You know, for someone so street wise, you sure are naïve as shit." He took another sip of his coffee, his reaction no more positive than from his first sip. "Man, they make some shitty coffee here."

He stared straight into Bridge's eyes, his hands gently pounding the table to emphasize his points. "Look, I'll level with you. We like to call ourselves journalists, and we ride that objective viewpoint pony until it is dead. But it's all bullshit. The more people I get staring at my face every night, the less actual journalism I'm allowed to do. I'm a glorified teleprompter with a dashingly handsome face, if I do say so myself."

He leaned back in the booth, a weary sigh escaping his body. "I'm not allowed to piss people off, I'm not allowed to make a stand, and I'm not allowed to break a story if the suits that give me my paycheck don't want me breaking it. At best, I get to regurgitate the talking points, the PR spin. Maybe once a year, maybe, someone with some actual journalistic abilities is allowed to get a page of copy to my desk and I get to read the truth before the bullshit is tossed on top of the body to cover it all up. I have a staff to do my legwork, which usually consists of emailing their plugged-in buddies to feed them the official lie."

"I'm the hype machine, buddy. It's a wonder I can still fucking dress myself."

Bridge sat aghast. "Jesus. I thought I was cynical."

"You ain't old enough to be this cynical, bucko," Tom smiled sardonically.

"So you won't even take this story for free then?"

"I don't even want to hear what it is. It'll just make me jealous." He took one last slug of coffee, and made a face that belonged on a poison control sticker. "Goddamnit, they gotta get some better coffee in here. Listen, I have to get back. We're doing a story on the glorious benefits the LGL has brought to Los Angeles." He seemed more intensely displeased over the story than he was the coffee. "Say, have you thought about using a leaker for the story? That's probably about the only way you're going to get it out there."

"Where do you think I got it from?"

Tom shrugged. "Well, good luck with that then. Once it gets out, I'd love to do a followup, if it's still news by the time you get it out." Bridge waved him off. "Suit yourself." Tom turned to leave, but Bridge stopped him.

"This doesn't all seem slightly suspicious to you, then? The eve of one of Los Angeles' biggest elections and you've been forbidden from breaking any story on the candidates. That doesn't smell at all fishy to you?"

Tom's sardonic smile was infuriating. "It stinks like last week's garbage. But it does alert my well-honed journalistic instincts to one thing." Bridge marveled that he could say those words with a straight face.

"Yeah and what's that?"

"The fix is in. Gird your loins, buddy." With that, the newsman left whistling some pre-21st tune.

Bridge sat and finished his meal, the wheels in his head turning desperately with every bite.

Chapter 9
August 30, 2028
1:14 p.m.

Bridge lingered long over an after lunch coffee, his mind in a tumult. In the best of circumstances, he would have had five paying options for selling this recording and moving on, but time was against him. Few would touch something this hot without demanding a serious discount for the added danger. Tom's intuition, for all its sarcasm, was spot on. There was definitely a fix in. Losman trying to pass Soto off as some kind of shining knight crusader might play well on the evening news but Bridge knew better. The network's sudden reluctance to break any sort of electionscandal just exacerbated his natural paranoia. The kind of high-level string-pulling this would require made his asshole twitch.

Soto had a reputation that Bridge was all too familiar with, even though he'd never done any business with the man. Soto had earned his reputation during the riots just like Bridge. Soto had lived in a lower middle class subdivision, not the type of place you'd see corporate types living in. Mostly Hispanic, it was populated by workmen, janitors, school teachers and retail workers, the kind of barely-above-the-poverty-level residents that politicians pandered to for elections before forgetting completely. He had been a struggling real estate developer living in the home his parents had bought back in the early '80's when home ownership was still attainable with hard work. The neighborhood had the unfortunate providence of being on the border between the poor areas that exploded into chaos during the riots and the targets of that chaotic rage, the downtown corporate sectors. It quickly found itself under siege, with rioters on one side wanting to march through the streets burning and looting everything along the way and the corporate cops on the other side trying to protect their employer's interests. Soto organized the neighborhood's defense, successfully fighting off both sides for days. When the LGL was passed, LAPD and the corporate cops were joined into one peacekeeping force which more often served as agents of corporate vengeance. Soto negotiated publicly with these forces to ensure their neighborhood was excluded from the overly violent pacification sweeps. As a result, his neighborhood was one of the least devastated areas in the city.

But Bridge knew a guy who lived there during the riots. Paco had cowered in his parents' basement most of the time, until Soto conscripted him. Paco hadn't wanted to fight, but Soto left him little choice, strong-arming the 17-year old into manning a barricade against the rioters. Paco had been a quiet hacker, the kind of kid that couldn't fight off swirlies in high school. When Soto was done with him, the kid was hard. The riots had done that to a lot of people, but Paco was a kid. He spoke about the things Soto had done, the murders he'd committed and the ones he'd ordered. Soto had been particularly brutal, at one point stringing up a rioter by his ankles and leaving him to die screaming yards in front of the barricades to discourage other invaders. Somehow, that brutality never made it into the official Soto story.

That made Bridge skeptical about the Soto campaign's desire for honor. Soto wasn't the kind of man who was squeamish about literally and figuratively crucifying his enemy when the situation called for it. His campaign manager having more scruples than her candidate was a nigh impossibility. The fix was in, but

Bridge was damned if he could figure out the angle.

Bridge paid for his meal and strode outside, not quite sure what his next move should be. He spotted a street term and logged in using another disposable ID to check his messages. The first six were all from Nicky, barely veiled threats at first, escalating with each successive call until the final message had lost all semblance of subtlety. Nicky was ready to put Bridge down, and had gotten pissed enough not to care that such a threat was being recorded. He was going to have to do something about Nicky, but that had to take a back seat to this Sunderland situation. He also had a message from that executive, Thames. The normally confident executive's voice sounded thin and frayed, and Bridge imagined his bosses were putting serious pressure on him. He'd have to wait as well. There was no way Bridge could stick his head out into the hacker pool far enough to hook up a leaker, not with a hit order floating around the GlobalNet. Aristotle had called to check up, and Bridge smiled a bit at the bodyguard's undeserved loyalty. Bridge really needed to give him a bonus.

The last message was from Stonewall, short and cryptic enough to make Bridge's heart skip a beat. "Yo, Bridge, give me a call about that thing, eh? I got news." Stonewall was really good at disguising his criminal activities with code words. Bridge immediately purchased another disposable ID and returned the call.

"Yo, Bridge, where you been?"

"Working another angle. You got something for me?"

"Yeah, but it ain't what you want. Louie Lou, eh?" The ex-footballer hung up without even a goodbye. That meant nothing good, and probably a whole lot of bad. The code words Louie Lou was a location where the two could meet.

Louie Lou was a restaurant on the decaying edge of the warehouse district, a shithole diner that saw more rendezvous traffic than regular diners. They had good coffee and crappy food, but if you needed to meet somewhere away from where the shit was going down, Louie Lou's was the place. Bridge caught a cab immediately, not even bothering to hide his trail. If Stoney wanted to meet at Louie Lou, it was an emergency.

Stonewall sat sipping coffee at a corner booth with a good view of the entire diner and the street outside. Catching sight of Bridge, he immediately dropped a few bills on the table and walked out. He greeted Bridge on the street with a curt, "Follow me." The lack of chit-chat made Bridge keep his mouth shut as they stalked west a few blocks into rows of warehouses. Three blocks into the walk and Stonewall started talking. "So we took your boy Paulie's crew to a safehouse and went to work on them. One of them didn't last the trip. The second one managed to make it all night. Poor bastard didn't talk though." Bridge had lost track of where exactly he was when Stonewall stopped at the side door of a large warehouse. The building was so dilapidated that Bridge at first thought it was abandoned. The key-pad entry was pristine, however, and the Mexican quickly entered a combination and opened the door. Bridge began to follow him in when he noticed the chaotic pattern of a shotgun blast in the dead center of the door. The door's metal was perforated, blackened holes at waist height giving Bridge a sinking feeling in the pit of his stomach. "Watch your step," Stonewall warned. Bridge narrowly avoided stepping directly in the puddle of blood on the floor. Whoever had been standing behind the door had taken the shotgun blast badly.

"We'd started working on Paulie when Twiggs sent me out for lunch. I was like ok, I'll pick up where my homies leave off. I couldn't have been gone half an hour." Stonewall led Bridge down a shadowy hallway. The blood from the puddle was smeared down the hallway, leading to a body face down in a pool of light. The coppery smell of bloody death seemed to soak the air in the warehouse, the air which was even now closing in on Bridge, so stuffy it was like breathing sawdust and paranoia and impending doom. He could feel the gorge rising in his throat while his back was awash in freezing sweat. Bridge began to say a vain prayer in hopes of warding off the inevitable scene he was about to witness.

"But this is what I found." Stonewall swept his arms wide to encompass the whole of the scene. The doorway opened into a tool storage area off of the main warehouse floor. A haphazard series of cheap metal shelves and cabinets containing various motor parts and tools formed a makeshift room around the doorway. It was well lit with burning incandescent spotlights hanging low from the ceiling. The air was stifling with the smell of settling dust, motor oil, sweat and blood. All the blood. Bridge felt his lunch start to revolt, heading back up his esophagus with sickening force. "Hold it in, hombre, you don't want the cops sniffing out your DNA 'cos you yak all over the crime scene." Bridge got a grip by steadying himself on one of the shelves, which wobbled under his weight. He drew back his hand from something sticky, but was relieved to discover oil on his hand instead of blood. He immediately grabbed a dirty towel from a nearby shelf and wiped both his hand and the shelf where he'd placed the hand. Stonewall approved. "Now you're learning."

"What the fuck happened?"

Stonewall surveyed the destruction nonchalantly. "You tell me, brother. Just who the fuck are... were these guys?"

Bridge began to study the scene carefully, reconstructing the interrogation in his head. The victim had been tied to a chair surrounded by three other chairs. Likely the questioner had sat directly across from the victim, the two flanking chairs holding the bruisers who would whale on the victim until he talked. One of the hanging lamps was low enough to be grabbed by the questioner but now swung in a faint elliptical pattern.

Various implements such as vice grips, pliers, knives and a blowtorch had been on a table to the right of the victim, a table that now held a bloody corpse. Bridge recognized the corpse as one of Twiggs' enforcers, Ernesto or Nester or something like that. The dead man's eyes were frozen open, a surprised expression framing the third eye blooming out of his forehead.

One of the metal shelves directly opposite the table was overturned. A pair of feet was visible, the landing point of another of Twiggs' employees. The chair to the left of the questioner's was also spilled, its occupant having flipped over onto his stomach from the force of the blast that had killed him. The final body was the most surprising. In the center of the circle of chairs lay Twiggs, flat on his stomach with his head turned to stare blankly at the light above him. The former striker had taken two large caliber bullets in the back, and a third to the base of his skull, likely both the killing blow and a message. Bridge let out a whispered curse and shot a glance at Stonewall. The enforcer just nodded, a grim nod suffused with a blinding finality. A queer look of melancholy crossed Stoney's face.

"Shit, Stoney, I'm sorry. I didn't..."

"Save it," the Mexican cut him off with a wave of his hand. "If it wasn't you, it was going to be somebody else got us all killed. Twiggs knew the type of bastards he was doing business with. He didn't promise me a long life, he promised me a job."

"You think this was a business hit?"

Stoney shook his head. "Not his business. His enemies would have left the two bodies." He pointed over his shoulder at an area of the warehouse floor where two separate blood stains sat drying in the dust. A piece of plastic film with bloody stains had been left nearby, probably having covered the two missing bodies. "That's where we put the ones didn't make it." Stoney pulled back the questioner's chair and sat with a sigh. He pulled out a pack of gum, offering a piece to Bridge who declined. Stonewall insisted silently, and Bridge took a piece with reluctance. "It'll settle your stomach," he said with a wry smile. Stonewall indicated that Bridge should sit.

Bridge sank into the chair with a vacant stare. His eyes caught sight of something by the victim's chair and he stared at it until he could comprehend it. Two fingers lay bleeding on the floor beside the chair. Bridge burped and barely covered his mouth with his hand, forcing the vomit back down with willpower alone. "Whose fingers are those?"

Stonewall blinked, said "Huh?" then found the digits Bridge was babbling about. "Oh, those. Probably Paulie's. We'd just started really working him over when Twiggs sent me out. Guess they figured he was harder than the other two."

"You notice something else?" Bridge shook his head. "No bullet casings."

"What's that mean?"

"Professional team, maybe even corporate. Thorough, but they knew how to make it look like a mob hit. Cops, maybe?" He shrugged. "We never could get a name out of them. Tough fuckers."

Stonewall leaned over to rest his elbows on his knees, the strangest expression of sadness on his face. Bridge could see something behind his eyes, a storm front of emotion building behind the rocky façade the enforcer put on. He stared down at Twiggs with that look in his eyes, squeezing his hands together until his knuckles turned white. "Did I ever tell you how I lost my knee?" Bridge shook his head. "It wasn't even in a goddamn game, just some training ground scrimmage shit. Twiggs was making a run right up the midfield, and I tackled him. Clean tackle, no funny business and I got possession. I'm heading back upfield, counterattacking right, gonna pass it off to… fuck, what was that guy's name?" He clapped his hands together as he remembered. "Ricketts, that was him. Pretty good winger. So I pass it off to him and here comes Twiggs from the side, studs up."

He sniffled a little, emotion getting the better of him as a solitary tear rolled down from his right eye. "I could feel the kneecap just ripping up, right? It totally shattered, pieces driven up into muscles and ligaments and shit tearing right up. Doctor's told me they could never reconstruct it as is, they had to use cybershit. Course, we all knew that would end it, what with FIFA being such dildos about warez. Twiggs apologized afterwards and you know what I told him? Same thing you always tell a footballer when he sideswipes you. I said, 'I'd have done the same thing, amigo.' I told him that, and every time we talked about it, I told him the same thing. No sense him feeling guilty about it, right? That's what you're taught, from a little dude, make the tackle and apologize afterwards. Never begrudge a man a tackle you'd have made yourself."

A raging thundercloud of anger erupted on Stonewall's face. His lips quivered. Something had broken free inside of him. "But that was a lie, dig? Only a fucking striker comes in with a tackle that dangerous. That shit would have got him a red in a game and he fucking knew it. He knew it, man. That's why he gave me this fucking job, that's why he always took care of me. You fucking knew it, didn't you! What was I, just some Catholic guilt you worked off? Did you feel good about yourself making me do all this shit? Did you? You know how many fucking bodies I buried? Yeah, neither do I and that scares the living shit out of me. But he just kept sending me out there. Stoney, crack this guy's jaw. Stoney, plant that deadbeat. And what'd it get you, eh puta? What'd it get you? It got you DEAD! Fuck you and burn in hell, you preppy shitbag! I'm glad you're dead!" Spittle flew off his lips as he screamed at the impassive corpse. His shoulders heaved and his breathing came in ragged gasps. His cathartic outburst over, he stood panting paying Bridge no mind whatsoever. Finally he composed himself, straightening his back and making the sign of the cross over his chest. "I'm glad you're dead," he said one more time with almost a whisper.

Catching Bridge's look of terrified embarrassment, Stonewall smiled. "That therapist you got me said I should work on releasing my anger in a non-violent manner. He's good."

"Should we be hanging around this slaughterhouse?"

Stonewall was about to speak, his mouth just opening to form the words when a beeping sound interrupted. He snapped to attention, darting over to an open doorway that led to a security room. Banks of monitors displaying feeds from various cameras all over the warehouse lined the walls. Bridge could see police cars pulling up in at least two of the exterior feeds. Stonewall cursed loudly. "We gotta get out of here," he said, springing into action. Slamming a button on the monitor console, he pushed Bridge out into the warehouse floor. The vehicle lift of one of the work bays began to rise, revealing the darkened pit of the oil changing bay below. "Somebody's called the cops on us, and unless you want to get framed for a gangster-style execution, it's time to beat feet."

The ex-footballer pushed Bridge down into the darkened bay, grabbing a shotgun, a pistol and some clips from underneath the vehicle lift as he did so. Bridge heard muffled shouts and the thwump of flash bang grenades behind him as he ducked below the level of the warehouse floor into darkness.

Chapter 10
August 30, 2028
2:03 p.m.

The darkness underneath the warehouse floor was stifling, rank with the smells of motor oil, sweat and dust. Bridge tried to get his eyes adjusted to the blackness but before he could, Stonewall turned on emergency lights with the flick of a switch. The enforcer must have been well-practiced at using this escape route, because Bridge would have stumbled in the dark for many minutes before locating that switch. The bay was bathed in a dull red light that turned it into a red-tinged nightmare of shadows. Stonewall moved with a practiced grace, his jaw set in determined, barely controlled anger.

"That way," he said curtly, pointing a finger behind Bridge. Bridge followed the finger, trying to discern where Stoney intended him to go. The room was a dead end, a blank series of four walls. It took a second to realize that what looked at first like an impenetrable wall was in fact a tiny alcove, the recessed exit built so as to be invisible except from close-up. Bridge started towards the alcove, tripping over the hydraulic apparatus lining the floor. "And take this."

Stoney tossed Bridge the pistol he'd grabbed from the hiding place underneath the bay. Bridge caught it awkwardly, barely grabbing the clip that followed. He spoke hesitantly. "I'm not really comfortable... I mean, I've shot one, but I've never actually shot anyone."

"And I don't suggest you shoot anyone now. Killing cops is a sure way to get the needle, even in this state. But you know, they got 'em, so you better have one just in case. Just don't shoot my ass and remember to take the safety off." The ex-footballer slipped through the crevice quickly despite his size, while Bridge had to wiggle a little to manage his way through. Behind the alcove was a long hallway with telecom pipes running both ways down the length of the dark corridor. Either end of the hallway was engulfed in shadow, the same red emergency lights providing the barest of illumination. Stonewall took an immediate left, flicking another switch as he passed. A small panel beside the alcove began to beep annoyingly. "We better vamoose."

"Where the hell are we?"

"Old 20th fiber trunks, built to wire this area up back in the '90's. Once Twiggs found out this place was right on top of them, he had this emergency exit built. Don't nobody use these tunnels much anymore 'less a cable breaks." The beeping sound started to fade away as the two adopted a brisk pace.

"What's that beeping?"

"You'll find out soon enough."

All Bridge could think of was explosives, and he quickened his step unconsciously. "Shit, you're gonna blow it up, aren't you?"

Stoney just flashed a mischievous grin. "Only a little piece."

Bridge could feel the tunnel veer a bit left, though he had long since lost any sense of direction. The tunnel filled with noise then, a cacophonous FOOOMPH followed by a shrill ringing in his ears. A thin coating of dust shook down from the ceiling, followed by a gigantic choking cloud that engulfed the entire tunnel. Bridge cursed loudly, though he couldn't hear his own voice over the ringing. His eyes watered from the dust and he coughed violently. Stonewall was talking to him, but he couldn't hear. He tried to focus on the man's mouth, tried to read his lips but to no avail. The Mexican had a hand on Bridge's arm and was trying to pull him down the corridor. Bridge started to follow when the ex-footballer raised the shotgun one-handed and pulled the trigger.

Bridge felt the shotgun blasts more than heard it, two quick vibrations shivering past his right arm. He looked back in the direction the shots had been fired, seeing a dark uniformed officer thrown to his back. The explosion had opened the alcove further, and Bridge thought he saw a few limbs buried under the rubble.

Another shadowed figure sprang from the hole in the wall, firing short, quick bursts from a submachine gun as he tried to make it across the tunnel, begging for cover that did not exist in the tight space.

Bullets whizzed past Bridge and Stoney, one coming close enough for Bridge to feel the wind displaced on his cheek. The brief flashes from the man's gun revealed a uniform with the letters SWAT emblazoned in white across the chest. Bridge threw himself backwards by reflex, raising the gun and firing wildly. He had squeezed off six shots by the time his back hit the ground, rolling over to face the attacker. None of the shots hit, but they were enough to send the target skittering down the hallway in search of cover.

Stonewall fired two more shots down the hall before yanking Bridge up violently by the arm. A little of Bridge's hearing had returned, allowing him to catch the gist of what the Mexican was telling him. It amounted to moving his ass and Bridge obeyed with the blood rushing in his head. Dizziness followed by nausea passed over him, but he maintained his balance and kept going. Stonewall pushed him around a soft bend to the left, which switched back to the right in a serpentine pattern.

Suddenly the tunnel exploded in light, brighter than the sun. Only the fact that Bridge faced away from the source saved his eyesight, but spots still danced in front of his eyes. The concussive force of the flashbang replaced what little hearing he'd gained back with a new piercing ringing. He cursed out loud, but kept moving.

Stonewall's reassuring hand still pressed on his back, pushing him forward, around corners, and through a bewildering maze of tunnels that so thoroughly disoriented Bridge that he could have emerged from the tunnels into the kingdom of the Mole People and not been the least bit surprised.

Finally, Stonewall yanked his shirt, stopping him cold. The Mexican said something to Bridge, but Bridge still couldn't quite hear it. The enforcer aimed his shotgun at one of the red lights illuminating the tunnel and blasted it, then took similar aim at lights to either side of the now darkened air and repeated his pinpoint shooting. Bridge was now thoroughly blind again, but Stonewall's hand on his arm pulled him towards where he knew the wall to be. Bridge reached out his hands blindly, his fingers touching cold metal instead of the expected stone. It was a door of some kind, and he fumbled around until he found a handle. The door opened inward, a sliver of yellow light briefly dispelling the darkness. Stoney pushed him through quickly, shutting the door behind him with silent care. He emptied the shotgun of shells and jammed it into the silver bar that opened the door on this side. It would take some major effort to open the door from the other side.

"Give... pistol..." Stonewall said, barely breaking through the ringing filling

Bridge's head. He handed over the pistol and clips eagerly. Stonewall checked the magazine, slamming it back into place forcefully before hiding the gun in the small of his back.

"Where the fuck are we?" Bridge asked.

Stonewall pointed at the ground where a pair of rails ran into the darkness in both directions. "Subway," he said gruffly. "They won't want to follow us down here."

"How do you know they won't?" Bridge asked, his vision starting to clear with only the occasional floater throwing off his balance. He felt the distant rumble of a train somewhere.

"Cops aren't coming into the subways anymore. They've given it to us."

"Us who?"

"The gangsters, the gangs. The criminals, the hobos, the naco. They've been giving this place up more and more since the corps took over." Stonewall pointed down the tunnel behind Bridge and started walking towards the barely perceptible speck of light. "Nobody takes the subway anymore. The rich got that new dirigible, the middle class got the taxis and the buses. The poor, they take the subway or they beat feet. Ain't no cops on the trains, hell, most stations don't even charge anymore. Haven't you noticed?"

Bridge shrugged, trudging along beside Stonewall. "I don't take the subway. My clients expect a certain style. I show up on the subway, they'll think I'm some kind of lowlife. Ok, some OTHER kind of lowlife. But why aren't the cops down here?"

"Have you just really not been paying attention to what these pendejos have been doing to this town?" Bridge shrugged again, and Stonewall scoffed. "I suppose you haven't noticed what they're turning the Warehouse District into either."

"I don't do business in the Warehouse District."

"That's right; you don't deal with the poor people, do you?" Stonewall said with an irritable disdain creeping into his voice. "You just get the *bourgeois* their dirty pleasures from the lower classes."

"You sound like some kind of communist."

"Just know how the world is, brother."

"Don't forget you're one of those *bourgeois*, brother."

"Yeah, I am." Stonewall's voice took on a wistful edge. "CLED's been busy since the LGL got passed. They call it pacification, settling down all the neighbor-hoods that are still resisting the whole LGL thing. That's bullshit, of course. Those riots ran out of steam once the food came back. But the CLED's got to show some progress, bring the crime rate down to prove the grand LGL experiment is a suc-cess. How do you think they pull that off? By moving the crime around like the queen in three-card Monty. They've been busy evicting folks from houses, pushing the drug trade and hookers and dice games and whatever else they can into the areas with the lowest crime rates. The crime rate in the hot spots goes down. Even if it goes up in other places, it averages out, see? And if you look hard enough, you can see where they are moving the worst of the worst. It's a series of lines that run the length of the subways. And all of 'em lead down here. They're creating their own little version of ethnic cleansing, their little invisible class war."

"How the hell did you get so political?" Bridge asked. He had a newfound respect for the footballer. He'd always thought of Stonewall as a typical superstar jock, a hardguy with little need for education. He'd probably underestimated the man by a mile.

"You think I'm just some dumb footballer, brother?" He shook his head. "You white guys, still think us Latinos are just lazy ass gangsters throwing down for our colors. My set went to college, motherfucker. Pumas didn't recruit me out of some Mexico City shithole, I got my degree in political science. I was gonna help the poor kids when I got done with soccer. I guess you never listened to Aristotle and me talking shit, did you?" Bridge shook his head. He noticed the ambient illumination growing with each step. The speck of light in the distance had grown taller and wider. They were nearing a station. "Course you didn't. That's a smart motherfucker. You should listen to him. Or at least, don't get him killed. We could use a smart brother like that. We're here."

Stonewall reached a hand up to the platform about chest high. Bridge was surprised to find a hand reaching down to help the footballer up onto the platform. He looked up to see three gang members with automatic weapons and tattoos up and down their arms offering to lift Bridge up along with Stonewall. The Mexican began speaking in hurried Spanish to the three. One began talking to himself, and Bridge figured he was speaking to someone on a cell connection. After a few minutes, Stonewall turned his attention back to Bridge.

"We got you a ride coming," he said flatly. "Take you into Downtown. Cops won't bother you there. You can also use the phones on the car, call anyone you want. It won't get traced. We've zeroed that bitch out. That line doesn't even exist in the records anymore." Bridge was impressed.

"You're not coming with me?"

Stonewall shook his head. "No, brother, Twiggs' boys are going to have some serious heat on them once that slaughterhouse gets searched. I expect the Arsenal is going to get hot pretty soon. I'm headed back to Mexico for a little while, lay low. Whoever you got me involved with, they got the power to fuck with us something fierce."

"Yeah, the mayor can do that," Bridge said. Stonewall didn't bat an eyelash.

"Figures. That fucker's in Chronosoft's pocket so deep, he's eating lint. I don't wanna know any more. Watch your ass, amigo."

"You too. I owe you, Stoney," Bridge said, trying to sound sincerely grateful.

"Save it. That thing you hooked me up with? Saved my life, whether you know it or not. We ain't square by a long shot." The platform filled with a rumbling sound, the train pulling into the station behind Bridge. "Castro here gon' see you safe," he said, indicating one of the three guards should accompany Bridge.

"Nobody will fuck with you."

Bridge shook his hand wordlessly then hopped on the train. Among the trash and gang tags littering the train, Bridge found a barely clean seat, trying hard to disguise his disgust at the accommodations. Castro didn't seem to notice or care. He leaned over a seat near the window, automatic weapon at the ready, one leg hiked up on the seat. Bridge noticed the tattoos on his left arm weren't tattoos, but decals covering the cybernetics like a sleeve. As the train got underway, he located the phone and began to make calls, a dangerous yet unavoidable plan forming in his mind. A ball of nervous resignation plummeted into his stomach as he settled on his next move.

Chapter 11
August 30, 2028
6:16 p.m.

Bridge had avoided this meeting as long as he could, but he had run out of acceptable options. If he couldn't sell the recording to Sunderland's opponent, if the news organizations wouldn't take it off his hands, he couldn't hire a leaker, and blackmail was untenable, he only had one other option. It was hardly preferable or profitable, but it had to be done. He made the first call to Angie, who passed on a message to Aristotle.

The bodyguard met Bridge in the lobby of the downtown Belker Hotel, mere blocks from the Chronosoft LGL Administrative Offices that had absorbed most of downtown since the riots. Combining the finest in modern amenities with architecture that hearkened back to the early '30's deco roots of the downtown Los Angeles area, the Belker was currently overrun with journalists and Sunderland campaign supporters. The mayor was due to speak to his adoring fans in less than an hour. As Bridge entered the opulent lobby, Aristotle approached him with a furrowed brow and a face full of worry. "Isn't this getting a bit too close to enemy territory?" he asked as he pulled Bridge around the corner from one of the large convention halls.

Bridge just gave his bodyguard a mischievous grin. "Business associates are never enemies," he replied with little conviction. He pulled a flower from the ornate vase sitting on a oak accent table, stuffing it into his lapel with aplomb. "What do you think? Too much?"

Aristotle nodded. "Just a bit too fruity for this crowd and that jacket. Didn't this business associate try to have you killed?"

"Allegedly. Look, I don't have much other choice. I try to blackmail this guy and I'm dead for sure. If he doesn't get re-elected, and that's 50/50 at best, he gets beat and the blackmail won't be worth shit. If I want anything out of this, I have to get rid of it in the next 24 hours. And since no one else is willing to pay a red cent, selling it back to its original owner is my best option, even if the only thing I get is to save my own ass. The worst he can do is try to kill me again and he's not going to do that with all this press around."

Aristotle did not look one bit reassured. "Did you bring it?"

Aristotle nodded and handed Bridge a bizchip. It was something Bridge had been sitting on for a while, a rainy day surprise he'd wheedled out of Tom Williams a few months back. Tom had given him press credentials in exchange for a voucher into a high-stakes card game. Tom really did have a problem. Of course, the credentials were shit, some kind of fluff entertainment reporter bullshit, but what the credentials lacked, Bridge would make up for with persuasion. "You're clear about what you're supposed to do?"

Aristotle nodded, but Bridge went over it again for good measure. "I get in here and try to work up an interview. I'll turn on my cell connection and let you listen in. Provided I actually get the interview, and I'm pretty sure I can, they'll probably white noise me. If you hear the connection cut out, you got five minutes to create as big a distraction as you can manage.

You realize you're probably going to get arrested, right?"

Aristotle shrugged. "All the greatest thinkers have been imprisoned for their political beliefs at one time or another. It will give me ample time to write."

Bridge's respect for the man grew a hundredfold. "You don't have to do this, you know. You can just head home right now, save yourself a night in the pokey. I wouldn't blame you a bit." Aristotle shook his head. "Why? It ain't like I'm the best boss in the world. Why are you sticking your neck out for me?"

Aristotle thought for a moment. He replied with the most matter-of-fact tone. "All this time, you've never treated me like a piece of meat. I'm your bodyguard, but you never ordered me to take a hit for you, not even a single punch. You'd rather take another beatdown than put me in harm's way."

"I can't afford a real bodyguard!" Bridge protested meekly, his cheeks flushing.

"Yeah, you keep on saying it. I know better." His smug smile was infuriating and encouraging at the same time. If Bridge got out of this, he'd need to do something for his employee, buy him something special.

"Angela has rented a car and will be waiting for us outside if we require immediate egress," Aristotle said.

Bridge's jaw set with painful anger. "What do you mean Angela's outside? She's offline? She's HERE?"

"Why yes, she insisted on coming along quite forcefully."

Bridge let out a string of curses. "Goddamnit, I didn't want her involved in this, especially in the flesh! What the hell is she thinking?" He reviewed his plans, trying to revise them to keep her out of harm's way. Finally, he said, "Look, whatever happens, do NOT let her get involved. I don't care if I'm about to get capped, you make sure she gets out of here even if I don't. You got that?"

"But Bridge, we can…"

"I mean it, Marcus. I don't want her in this." Bridge's use of Aristotle's real name obviously affected the man, and he nodded his assent grudgingly. "All right, how do I look?" Bridge asked as he straightened his tie in the nearby mirror.

"Like five miles of deteriorated road," Aristotle replied with gallows humor. "The bruises are a bit obvious."

He was right, Bridge looked a mess. Despite his practiced attempts at concealing the damage with makeup, both eyes sported nasty shiners, his lip was split and his clothes were rumpled. One glance at his appearance brought the fatigue of the day into sharp focus, his shoulders slumping with the stress. "Nothing to be done about it now. The speech is about to start." Bridge buttoned his coat and strode purposefully towards the convention room brandishing his fake press passes. He half-expected them to be rejected, ending his potentially suicidal gambit, but the guards just shuttled him quickly through with barely a glance at his disheveled condition. 'Political reporters must get their asses beat constantly,' Bridge thought to himself sardonically.

As he entered the darkened room, the buzzing hum of conversation died to an awkward whisper. The large hall held probably two hundred or so, and it was packed to the gills with reporters from local, national and international venues. The room was lit by several spotlights focused on the stage, festooned with various campaign materials bearing the slogan "Into the Bright, Shining Future." A speaker was introducing the Mayor, praising the politician's dedication to rebuilding the city. Bridge quickly tuned out. He shuffled as quietly as he could into the crowd, searching for the kind of reporter he knew would be in attendance. He was looking for the cynic, the guy so sick to death of the whole political dog and pony show, the guy who'd talk to anyone about anything so long as the cynicism was mutual. In the end, he spotted his man on the fringes of the room, leaning against the wall with a scotch in one hand and a microphone held lazily towards the stage in the other. This was Bridge's guy.

Bridge sidled up next to the cynic with casual indifference, offering a greeting in the form of a head nod. The cynic returned it with little sincerity. Bridge leaned over with a convivial quip, noting the reporter's name on his badge as Cary Batson from Channel 17. "I wonder which talking points he'll hammer tonight."

The cynic offered him a sheet of paper with the campaign letterhead in holographic letters at the top. "Didn't you get the memo? He's going for all of them."

Bridge indicated the microphone held by the cynic. "Isn't that thing going to catch all this?"

"This? Not likely. It's not even on. But if you don't at least look like you're doing something, the jackboots start giving you shit. I could have done this remote yesterday from memory." They shared a schoolboy level chuckle, and then turned their collective attention back to the stage where the introduction had been completed. The mayor bubbled out onto the stage, the applause from his supporters fervent with screaming and clapping while the journalists offered polite golf claps while trying to look interested.

Sunderland looked more corpulent and slimy in person than he did on his commercials, a pudgy man with a lilting, effeminate voice that spoke of nothing so much as concessions and beliefs that shifted with those of his audience. Bridge couldn't think of a less palatable candidate for any sort of position of responsibility, though he certainly could chalk that up to having seen the mayor's disgusting cybersexual display. The speech began with disingenuous thank-you's for support and encouragement, and continued with clockwork precision along the talking points sheet. The whole thing had the flavor of a pantomime as well-rehearsed as Bridge's introduction speech to his clients. He got the sense of the politician's greater role as the official state fixer, the go-to guy when you need something no one else can get. Was that all government really was? A series of handshakes and handouts based on an arbitrary series of rules that at least had the benefit of being codified, as opposed to the extra-legal series of unwritten rules that Bridge bumped up against daily? Here was Sunderland's promise to the land developers to grease the wheels of government to make sure the economy recovered. There was Sunderland's offering to the authoritarians in attendance to protect them from street violence. With a flourish, he offered to lower property taxes and increase services.

The mayor was just another bridge, a trader of favors with an official title and the backing of legal enforcers.

Bridge shook himself from his thoughts and leaned over to Cary with a whisper. "So has anybody been able to get an interview with the man himself?"

"Sure, if you've been kissing the right asses. Mitzy over there," he indicated an attractive blonde mouthpiece with legs up to her neck, "she got the exclusive a week or so ago. Word is Breckin has a thing for the blondes."

"Breckin?"

"Yeah, Breckin Sims, the mayor's press watchdog. He's the guy you suck up to if you want a little face time, and he's the guy who snaps off your dick if you start fucking around." Cary arched his neck as he scanned the faces in the room. "There he is," he continued, pointing out a sharply-dressed corporate PR type watching the stage with a bemused reverence. "Of course, you'll never get one, not this late. The less unrehearsed speaking the mayor does this close to the election, the happier Breckin gets."

"My nuts are in a wringer. My editor says if I don't get something with the mayor, my desk is cleaned."

"Good luck with the unemployment line then, buddy," Cary said with a rueful laugh. Bridge crossed his fingers to the cynical reporter and walked off, stalking deliberately towards the PR gatekeeper. The police escorts guarding the entrances to the stage flinched as Bridge approached, their eyes locked on his path.

"Mr. Sims? Caston Bocanegra," Bridge began, flashing his fake credentials with the same air of confidence he used on his clients. "I'd like to speak with the mayor, maybe get a five minute interview if I could."

"I'm sorry, Mr. ... Bocanegra did you say? The mayor's schedule is booked solid until the election. I can't even squeeze Tom Williams in these days, much less any fluff reporter, no offense." The man's smile was so white his teeth gleamed with reflected spotlight, and his attitude had the galling arrogance to match.

"But I have some very important questions about the mayor's campaign. If I could just get three minutes with the man..."

"Three minutes is more than he has to offer. I'm very sorry."

"Just tell him that I have a story about Candy. He'll know who I'm talking about. Candy. Remember that. If he still wants to talk after the speech, I'll be over there." Bridge pointed to the open bar across the room, currently occupied by a swarm of disinterested reporters. He floated towards the bar hiding the smug smile from the PR man. Despite the danger, or maybe because of it, he was enjoying this entirely too much. The last look he'd gotten at Sims' face was priceless, the barely-concealed fear of a man who'd just been told his meal ticket was getting punched.

The speech was interminably long, a series of regurgitated buzzwords and catchphrases that said nothing much in particular with a preponderance of words. Bridge admired the man's ability to promise absolutely nothing while managing to make it seem like the moon was being offered to the crowd in exchange for their votes. Bridge nursed a couple of whiskeys during that time, engaging in meaningless chit-chat with some of the other reporters. A few he'd heard of through his association with Tom Williams, others he'd seen while flipping through channels. The disparity between the on-air personalities and the actual reporters was striking, and not just in their looks. The talking heads managed to pull off the appearance of genuine interest, while the less attractive jotted an occasional note on a PDA between irritated glances at their watches. Finally the speech ended with a flourish of applause, and the mayor left the stage, his politician's smile fading as quickly as he left the spotlight's glare. Bridge watched the pudgy man stride off stage and past Sims, who stopped the mayor with a hand, whispering in his ear with furtive, conspiratorial glances around the room. Bridge could tell the minute Candy's name was mentioned, as the mayor's face grew stormy, a red flush of anger darkening the man's otherwise stoic demeanor. Sims pointed in Bridge's direction, and the mayor almost exploded, sticking a furious finger into the PR man's chest. With cowed resignation, Sims nodded to the mayor and walked off towards Bridge, while the mayor exited the room flanked by uniformed and plain clothes protectors.

"Congratulations, Mr. Boncanegra, the mayor has five minutes for you after all. If you'll come with me?" Bridge nodded, replacing his half-empty glass on the bar and following behind Sims. He activated his cell connection to Aristotle as they walked through a door on the opposite side of the room from the mayor's exit. Sims led them around a few corners and into the kitchen area of the hotel. Bridge had to squeeze past waiters and carts stacked with trays of dirty dishes.

As they turned the corner into a pantry area, Bridge was floored by a shot to the solar plexus, a well-trained blow that forced all the air out of his lungs and dropped him to his knees. His assailant was a large man in a plain dark suit, its cheap stitching stretched by the man's effort. His other fist struck Bridge across the cheek, the metal knuckles scraping a gash on Bridge's face. He was knocked onto his side.

"That's enough," said the lilting voice of the mayor. "We don't want to kill him." Bridge peered up into the faces of four men: the mayor, two almost identical bodyguards and Sims. "You can go, Breckin."

"Yes, sir," replied Sims, exiting the room with nervous glances at the body-guards. He obviously had no taste for the hard realities of the situation.

"Remember we have to press the flesh in five."

Sunderland waved a dismissive hand in Sims' direction. "Yes, yes, now beat it." The mayor hiked up his pants as he squatted down to look Bridge in the eye. "Now you listen here, you little shit. What the fuck game are you playing at?"

Bridge checked his cell connection on his HUD, amazed that it still connected. Something wasn't right about that. The bodyguards hadn't checked Bridge for any sort of wire; he hadn't had his goons deaden any transmission away from Bridge with portable white noise generators. Those things were cheap enough that Bridge carried one around with him. Either this guy was the most idiotic criminal on the planet, or he just didn't give a damn about getting caught doing naughty things.

"No game, your honor," Bridge said around gasps for air. "I have the recording your guys are looking for. I'm willing to give it to you, cheap."

Sunderland's head bobbed around as he looked from bodyguard to bodyguard. "You little bastard. You're trying to squeeze me? ME? You're trying to squeeze me for more money? That wasn't the deal. You don't just go off script on this thing here, you stick to the plan. I'm not paying you one goddamn cent for that shit. You got your paycheck when we started this thing." Bridge's mind kicked into overdrive. He'd miscalculated somewhere. Had Kira been blackmailing Sunderland? That didn't make sense. The hacker wouldn't have tried to get rid of his only ammunition, for free no less, if he had this guy on the hook already. If Kira had even half a brain, Sunderland would never have known who he was, and couldn't have sent someone after him. Kira may have been young and socially clueless, but he wasn't stupid.

Bridge raised a hand to forestall any more beating. "Wait, wait, I think we've come to a misunderstanding here. I'm not trying to blackmail you. I'm just trying to return your property what got stolen from you. The recordings fell into my possession when you sent your guys around to recover them."

"My guys? I didn't send any guys around. Are you telling me those fuckers lost the recordings? Shit, I said that guy was too young to be handling an operation

113

like this. Now I'm going to have to be the one clean it up."

Something dark and cold began to form in Bridge's mind. This was a man with no concerns. He knew good and damn well this career-destroying information was floating out in the wild. He was in no way concerned about possible electronic eavesdropping despite being embroiled in the most important election of his life. This man had no qualms about popping a cap in Bridge's ass with the press mere yards away. Even worse, Paulie and his crew weren't in Sunderland's employ, which meant one pissed off ex-footballer with two missing fingers was out there looking to steam roll Bridge. He was going to have to do some serious soft shoe to get the fuck out of danger. "Wait, wait, I have the recordings. Or I can get them at least. You don't even have to pay me, see? I'll just give them to you. Wash my hands of the whole thing. Call it even."

Sunderland's doughy face chewed over that thought a moment before replying. "Like I need that kind of trouble. Boys, you know what to do." Sunderland began to shamble out of the pantry, putting his hands absentmindedly in his jacket pockets. Bridge's eyes darted around in a panic, desperately searching for some way out. From a distance, he began to hear a high-pitched keening wail, building in intensity from down the crowded hallway. A tray crashed to the ground with a metallic clanging. Just as Sunderland stepped into the hallway, a flash of black skin blew past him, his red tie flapping above him. With chagrined relief, Bridge recognized the buck naked form of his bodyguard.

Aristotle was saving his ass again. The man had stripped to the skin and sprinted into the kitchen. He'd grabbed the mayor's tie on the way past, discombobulating the fat politician. As the bodyguards rushed towards the door, the fire alarm blared into life, the sprinklers erupting with a gushing hiss, showering the tiny room with stale water. At the height of the confusion, Bridge struck, mentally crossing his fingers that neither guard had metal legs. He kicked out at the nearest kneecap, hitting it squarely from the side. A sickening pop echoed in the tight space and Bridge pressed his advantage, upending a heavy metallic shelf full of food, spices and pots onto the guards. Though his side was on fire from the beatings he'd taken in the last few days, pure adrenaline propelled him as he shouldered past the guards. He knocked the mayor for a loop, sending the pudgy politician reeling in soaked confusion. He cut down the hallway Aristotle had come from, hoping that the guards would be focused on cutting off the first threat's exit. Bridge took one corner, and then another, ducking behind a wall just as more of the mayor's body-guards went past him towards the disturbance.

The key to getting out of the building now was to move quickly without appearing hurried, blending into the evacuating throng. He hoped like hell the guards and policemen swarming around the hotel were more interested in the streaking naked black man than the beat up but well-dressed white guy. Bridge passed a few frantic guards with little incident and had even begun to relax in a crowd of moderately-panicked reporters when a trio of guards standing between the door and Bridge spotted him. Scenarios shot through Bridge's mind as he continued to walk calmly towards them. Beyond the doors, he could see Angela's car idling. If she'd seen him, he just had to get to the car and she'd have the door open. The windows all around the lobby area were inviting targets, but Bridge reconsidered trying to make a mad crashing escape through them.

A hotel this posh would likely have bulletproof glass, especially one that hosted big political events such as tonight's speech. There were a few side exits, but he'd have to walk around the front of the building in plain sight offering ample opportunity for interception. He couldn't really run towards the door anyway, not without jostling the crowd around him making himself even more conspicuous. He was just going to have to bull his way through. His spirit sank.

Ten feet from the guards, Aristotle came roaring out of the bar behind the guards, crashing into them with bubbling laughter. The four men rolled over in a heap and Bridge took advantage, hopping over the pile of arms and legs and bursting through the door into the oppressive summer heat. Angela's eyes grew wide and she quickly reached over to open the door. As Bridge began his dive into the front seat, Angela threw the car into drive, blasting away from the hotel with shrieking tires. Bridge barely got the door closed behind him before she turned the corner, throwing him haphazardly around the cabin with a painful thump.

Bridge sighed, finally relaxing. His breath coming in ragged gasps, he said, "What... the hell... are you... doing here?"

"Saving your ass, baby," she said with that puckish grin beaming on her face. "Saving your ass. Be grateful and shut it."

Bridge did just that, exhaustion finally overtaking him as he slumped back against the seat.

Chapter 12
August 30, 2028
8:49 p.m.

The only discussion during the ride to Angela's place was Bridge's breathless suggestions for the route home. His paranoia was now well and truly in gear, and he sent them all over the Los Angeles area in the most circuitous route possible to throw off any pursuit. By the time they reached Angela's apartment complex, he was absolutely exhausted. His limbs felt like solid lead, and he moved with a languid, almost drugged pace. Angela parked the car close to her apartment over his feeble objections, but he was inwardly grateful for the short walk up to her place despite his protestations. He leaned heavily on the wall as she opened the door, then stomped straight to the couch and practically collapsed, sinking back into the cushions with a grunting sigh and closing his eyes.

He just had nothing left in his tank. All his plans had gone to shit. There was no one to sell the recording to, and no profit to be made from the venture. He was likely going to be on the lam from the police as soon as the mayor's people put a name to his face. His bodyguard was likely in lockup and bailing Aristotle out would cost Bridge all the money he had if he could even show his face at the station without getting arrested on sight. And on top of all that, he had a puzzle he couldn't figure out. Sunderland not only wasn't surprised about the recording, he was well aware of it. There had been some sort of plan for that information, something that required Kira's talents.

The politician had planned on Kira getting hold of that recording, and doing something with it. Since Kira was a leaker, it was safe to assume Sunderland had wanted the recording leaked. But why would a politician knowingly record a career-killing indiscretion on the eve of the most important election of his life? Was he politically suicidal? Was he just plain fucking nuts? Something was missing, some piece of information Bridge had not seen yet that would put it all together, but Bridge was too exhausted to even speculate on what that could be.

He wasn't sure how long he'd sat there dozing half asleep, his mind racing over and over the same ground. His eyes snapped open as Angela took a seat beside him, plopping down forcefully while flipping the television on. "You really don't look good," she said playfully. Bridge gave her a half-grin, half-grimace.

"It's been that kind of a day."

She noticed the drying blood on his cheek. "You know you're bleeding, right? You sure you shouldn't go to the hospital?" She leaned over and touched the gash gingerly, her hand brushing up against his ribs. He winced painfully. "Was that your ribs? Are they broken?"

"No, they're not broken. I know what broken feels like."

A previously undiscovered set of matronly instincts suddenly appeared. "All right, that's it, off with the shirt. I want to see this." He gave her a stubborn look of refusal, but she was having none of it. "I mean it, off. If I think your ribs are broken, I'm taking you to the fucking emergency room if I have to drag you by the stubble on your chin. Let's go!" He knew Angela's innate stubbornness. She wasn't going to be shifted without violent words he was entirely too exhausted to muster up. The concern in her voice was surprisingly alluring.

"Fine, fine." He threw off his jacket, pulled his tie over his head and unbuttoned the top three buttons on his silk shirt before pulling it over his head. The movement robbed him of any breath, his ribs a fiery bundle of pain. "See, I'm a lovely shade of black and blue."

"Goddamn, Bridge, how the fuck did you manage to get that many bootheels on your sides?" From just under his right armpit down to his hip, splotches of blue, black and yellowed skin tattooed his torso with a roadmap of pain. The other side wasn't much better. He even had a shoe pattern scrape on his stomach that was scabbing up nicely, a wound he attributed to Paulie. "Sit right there, don't move." She ran to the kitchen and began banging through cabinets and drawers. He heard the water running for a moment, but didn't bother to look around. He stared glassy-eyed at the television, which was running some nature program about coyotes or hyenas in the desert. He wasn't paying enough attention to be sure of the species other than it was some kind of canine.

She returned to the couch with a wet rag, a bottle of rubbing alcohol, a bottle of vodka, cotton balls and a few bandages. "I'm not good at this, but sit still and I'll have you taken care of," she said sternly. He just shrugged. Her first move was to the rubbing alcohol, pouring it on a cotton ball before jabbing it straight into the cut on his face. She ignored his loud curses. "Shut it, you big baby. It can't hurt that badly. Be good, and I'll get you a lollipop." He flipped her the bird with a rueful smile. "No lolly for you!"

She covered the gash with a bandage, then handed him the vodka. "Here, take a slug of that. Better than aspirin." He chuckled and took a big hit from the bottle.

"What, no bourbon?" he said after swallowing with a grimace.

119

"That's you that drinks that shit, not me. I'm a vodka woman." She ran gentle hands over his midsection, testing for breaks. He winced again and again as she prodded him, but the activity seemed to satisfy her concerns. "Well, it looks like you're right, nothing's broken."

"I did tell you," was his sarcastic reply.

"And I told you to shut it. I'd rather it hurt for a minute than you die on my couch." She finally noticed the program he was watching. "What you watching?" Two coyotes were fighting viciously, biting and growling and scratching with passionate venom. The scene cut to the end of the battle, with the loser limping off and the victor raising a leg to mark his territory. "That poor doggie!"

Bridge chuckled. "That's nature for you. It's not like that's all that different from us. We're all just fucking dogs, running around trying to mark our territory so somebody will know we were here, what we did was important. Just pissing in the wind, don't mean nothing. We're all just waiting around for a bigger dog to come steal our shit." Angela just rolled her eyes.

"Wow, aren't we philosophical tonight?"

"Almost getting a bullet in my brain pan in some hotel kitchen pantry gets me a little metaphysical, know what I'm saying?"

"Yeah, that's you, the big philosopher. What the hell happened, Artie? You used to want to create something, something big and beautiful and new.

You always talked about building a virtual world to get away from the shit. What happened to that guy?"

"That guy saw too much. That guy didn't realize how many people out there are just waiting to crack him over the skull for a fiver. When it all comes down, it's every man for himself."

His answer seemed to bring down her mood. He caught the barest hint of a wistful sadness in her eyes before she looked away. "We aren't all out to get you, Artie. Hell, Aristotle got busted tonight to keep you from getting killed. That's got to be worth something."

Bridge took another swig, wiping his lips with the back of his hand. He scowled at the bottle, replaced the cap and put it on the bare coffee table. "Yeah, I'll get him something good. If I don't get whacked that is."

Her gaze returned to him, and the sadness was gone. In its place was a familiar expression, something Bridge didn't expect to see there again. All the signals were written on her face plain as day. "Well, if you're going to get whacked, you should at least spend your last night doing something worthwhile." Her smile was pure sex, and Bridge found himself responding in kind.

She leaned over and kissed him slowly at first, but with growing intensity, taking care not to put any weight on his injuries. She quickly shifted on the couch to straddle him, grabbing his hand and leading it to the right place. They made out for a few minutes this way, her shirt ending up piled on top of his. All the fatigue seemed to drain out of his body. Somewhere in between breathless kisses, he asked about her Korean boyfriend. She shrugged it off with an absentminded, "Seoul is a long way from here" before engaging Bridge in another passionate kiss.

She stopped suddenly, pulling away from his lips. Her expression had a seriousness that surprised him. "This don't mean nothing, understand?"

He pondered it for a moment and nodded. "It never does."

Bridge slept like a stone, any dreams he had lost to post-coital exhaustion. He certainly couldn't have said it was his best performance, but given the circumstances, he thought he acquitted himself well enough. Angela seemed to respond with equal excitement, and they both fell asleep with enthusiastic yet silent cuddling. Bridge was thankful for the silence. He wasn't sure of his feelings about this lapse. Better to avoid that discussion at least until the morning.

His consciousness returned with syrupy slowness. Angela had moved quietly beside him and he lay with eyes closed, trying desperately not to wake fully. His mind struggled to remember whose bed he lay in, and he mumbled incoherently. Slowly, he came to realize that someone was watching him, and he muttered, "Go 'way, sleeping." The presence didn't move and he smiled, picturing Angela sitting over him watching like she used to. Finally, he cracked open an eyelid and found himself looking up into one ugly mug.

"Wake up, sunshine," said Paulie, a cruel smile plastered on his ghastly face. His lip was split, both eyes were horribly bruised and various cuts and bruises littered the craggy landscape of his already undesirable visage. Bridge tried to get up, his only reward a short jab to the chin for his troubles. "Ah ah, Polly, no sense running off just yet. We've brought you breakfast in bed, we 'ave." He fed Bridge another helping of knuckles and smiled a toothy grin.

Paulie grabbed Bridge's throat with his left hand and pressed Bridge into the bed with a suffocating strength. He held up his right hand, displaying the empty area his middle and ring finger had previously occupied. "Now see, normally this would be your arse, mate. This is a right big debt you owe me and if I 'ad me way, the last thing you'd see before your eyeballs popped out of your 'ead would be my pretty puss." The enforcer squeezed even harder to prove his point. Bridge's vision began to swim, spots dancing in front of his eyes as his consciousness ebbed. Just as suddenly as it had started Paulie let loose of his throat. "But that ain't the job." Coughing violently, Bridge almost fell out of bed.

"So let's talk then," Paulie said, sitting down on the bed and scratching the beginnings of a scruffy beard. Bridge saw past him to his helpers, two gigantic sides of beef with cybershades and long coats. One held Angela with a gloved hand covering her mouth. Her eyes were wide, a mixture of fear and anger. They had at least let her get dressed it appeared, though her feet were bare. "You 'ave been a very naughty boy," Paulie began. "See, that recording you've been trying to peddle about town, that's not yours, now is it? No, no it is most certainly fucking not. Your little hacker buddy, he 'ad a job to do, see? But instead of doing that job that he was well-paid for, he fucked right off. So when he disappeared, we figured he'd try to get rid of the thing. And who better to give it to than you? If he'd 'ave just done the job, he'd still be alive."

Paulie looked over at Angela with a disdainful expression. "Come this time tomorrow, your little girlfriend will be in the same boat as Kira if we don't get what we want. And so will you if I get my way. But, if you're really good, you can avoid all that. You know what we want?" Paulie stopped talking and stared at Bridge, who nodded with angry intensity.

"You want the recording leaked."

Paulie snapped the fingers of his left hand. "Eureka, mates, I think he finally gets it. You see that?" He snapped his fingers again. "I used to be able to do that with both hands, and thanks to you and your little Spic friend, now I'm half a snapper. I gotta go and get some metal fingers now. I'm betting those fingers snapping is gonna sound like a fucking steel drum. For that, we will be settling up once this is over. But for now, yes, we want that recording leaked to as many places as it can be by 7 p.m. this evening or your little girlfriend is snuffed. And then I come after you. Do it, boys."

The enforcer standing next to Angela pulled out a skinpatch and stuck it on her neck. She fought for a second before slumping against her captor. She was conscious but had become overtly pliable, a glassy-eyed stare on her face and a languid droop to her limbs. The patch must have been Sluv, the latest frat boy date rape drug. It left the victim conscious and aware, but completely malleable to the whims of anyone who could catch her attention. The enforcer sat her down and put shoes on her, then led her out the door.

"7 p.m. Start the seeding by then or she's done for. Got it?" Bridge nodded his assent.

"Where do I pick her up once it's over?"

Paulie reached into his coat and withdrew a bizchip. "This address. Bring proof or well, you know." He tossed the chip on the bed. "Now, you don't want her back, you just head off. She's a bit skinny for my tastes, but she'll do, eh?" Paulie began to walk out the door.

"Hey Paulie," Bridge said. The footballer stopped in the doorway. "This is over, you won't need to look for me." The man just smiled that toothy grin again, tipped an imaginary hat to Bridge and walked out chuckling.

That was it, then. Bridge knew what was required. The recording was supposed to be leaked. Traditional news organizations had little real credibility with scandal stories they generated, but leaked media like this could be believed. The mainstream news would pick it up, replaying hours and hours of hurried interviews, talking heads and paid experts to expound on the story, all without looking like scandalmongers. Soto's people got to benefit from the scandal without seeming like mudslingers. And the mayor, the mayor got his career ruined, something he was perfectly happy with by all appearances.

That was the part Bridge couldn't quite figure out yet. Sunderland was trying to throw the election, and Soto and the media were in on it. The fix was in, but why would a guy like Sunderland willingly give up the job? What did he get out of it? As Bridge puzzled over the scenario, he picked up the bizchip. His teeth clenched together so hard they hurt.

Bridge had seen the bizchip before. He already had a copy of Thames' card, and it was the last thing he'd expected to get from Paulie. A slow-building fire of anger smoldered in his stomach as he realized he had been played. For a fleeting moment before he'd picked up the card, he had thought about bagging it all in, packing up and getting the fuck out of LA with his ass intact. Screw Angela, screw Aristotle, screw all this political bullshit.

But it was personal now. He'd been played. It was time to fight back.

"You want me to do what?" The indignant surprise in Gina Danton's voice made Bridge cringe a bit despite himself. Bridge sat with the CLED patrolman in her personal car, parked in the deserted parking lot behind the MacArthur Park subway station. Trash blew by the car as a dusty wind picked up from the direction of Westlake Avenue. The parking lot was deserted at this early hour. A few pedestrians came and went on the streets, but none took notice of the parked auto. Bridge had insisted she not roll up in a CLED vehicle. He threw a few nervous glances towards the subway station, where some of the gang members who ran the subway kept a lookout for anyone brave enough to enter the station. They certainly noticed the car, but were polite enough to act like they weren't watching its occupant's every move.

"I need you to bail Aristotle out of jail," Bridge repeated patiently.

"I heard you the first time. I just wanted to make sure you had actually lost your mind and it wasn't me losing my hearing." Danton really was a looker out of uniform. Her silky blonde hair flowed over her shoulders, a much sexier do than the tight bun she sported on duty. A little makeup did wonders for her already attractive face, and civvy attire flattered her tight curves and well-toned body much better than the uniform. But no matter how she was dressed, the hardness of her character infused her every word. It wasn't just the job that made her an ice queen. She was just naturally tough, a stoic core of stone wrapped in a pretty shell. "You realize that just talking about pulling favors as simple as fixing a ticket can get us both arrested by IA, right?"

"I do realize that. Look, we both know that no matter how many changes the suits force on you, police work hasn't really changed. Without a smoking gun, you need one bad guy to drop dime on the other bad guys. You trade favors for that kind of information all the time. That's the way it's done."

"What are you telling me, Bridge? Are you ready to drop dime?" Bridge said nothing, letting the rather unkempt state of his person tell her all she needed to know about his level of desperation. "I don't think you understand just how much these Chronosoft guys have changed things. We got more paperwork than ever before, and every single nano-penny is counted, tracked, stamped and audited. Believe it or not, those suits have actually improved the place. We still got some of the old asshole Neanderthals trying to keep up business as usual, but the writing's on the wall. That old school skull cracking alpha male bullshit is out. I'd almost say the place is professional. I may not like the suits, but they have cleaned that place up."

"And the one thing suits understand is the art of the deal," Bridge said with a crooked grin. "They know dollars and cents, and they know public relations. And big busts make good public relations. All they've got to do is release a guy who doesn't even have a record."

"Aristotle's got a record."

It was Bridge's turn to be surprised. "Marcus? Marcus has a record?"

"Oh yeah. I guess you didn't interview him all that well, but then you probably don't believe in background checks, do you? No, he's got priors, most of it petty assault, low-level gang shit. That's why I was kind of glad he hooked up with you. I thought you'd keep him out of that shit." Her disappointment was smeared across her face. Bridge had let her down, and he hadn't even known it.

"Huh, I never knew. He didn't talk about it."

"He was always smarter than that. But once you got that stink on you, going legit is hard. Nobody reputable wants to hire you."

"I hired him."

"See what I mean? Nobody reputable." She was only half-joking, but Bridge mocked offense just the same. They didn't call him the Amoral Bridge for nothing. "You put him through college and I THOUGHT you'd keep him from getting in fights. Now you got him arrested again. What did he do?"

"Saved my goddamn life," Bridge mumbled ruefully. "It's a minor beef, unless they embellish it. All he did was streak the hotel after the mayor's speech, set off a false fire alarm. Oh and he stumbled over some guards that were in my way. He could always say it was a frat pledge thing."

Danton just buried her head in her hands with a disgusted sigh. "Goddammit, Bridge, the fucking mayor? Could you get him in any more trouble? Can I at least ask why?"

"Not if you want to help him," Bridge replied. "The less you know about why he did what he did, the better."

Danton mulled it over for a minute, leaning over to rest her chin on the steering wheel. "Look at those two," she said, pointing out the subway guards. "Do they really think I don't know what they're doing? I'd bust their asses myself if I had probable. People ought to be able to use the goddamn subways." Her rambling seemed to be to no one in particular, a distracted lilt to her voice that masked her internal struggle. Finally, she came to a conclusion.

"What are you offering me?"

Bridge clapped his hands and rubbed them together.

"Something juicy. Two days from now, there's going to be a big-time hold up, and I know whose going to pull it off."

"And how exactly do you know this?" Bridge's smile told her she didn't want to know. "Because you're going to set up the score, of course. Fine, fine, go on."

"Remember that guy whose boys were giving me the beatdown the other night outside the Glitter?"

"Sharver? You're gonna give me Sharver? He's not exactly film at 11 material."

"He's big enough for what I'm getting in return. Now do you want him or not?"

She nodded reluctantly. Bridge began to spill the beans, giving the entire setup for Nicky's proposed heist. He had already lined up the hacker replacement Nicky had so violently requested. Of course, the hacker was dead. Bridge had used the ID of the one that had tried to assassinate him. But Nicky didn't know that, and there was no reason to sell one of Angela's guys down the river when a little creative running had given Bridge the opportunity to set Nicky up. Bridge would get rid of one troublesome contact, and if he got lucky, he'd do it without Nicky knowing who had set him up. And even if Nicky did find out, Bridge would deal with that problem when it came up.

Aristotle would be safe. Now Bridge just had to do the same for Angela.

Bridge's next meeting was much more difficult to arrange than his morning's rendezvous with Gina Danton. It only took him three hours to set up, because he was just that good, but it was a close run thing. In the end, he'd had to come clean about the danger Angela was in, and it was only because of Angela's reputation among the LA hackers that Bridge even had a chance. One didn't just meet Michael Freeman these days, not in the flesh.

Freeman was a legend, an icon of the LA hacker scene from the good old days. He was the old man of the movement. He'd been living on the net since before there were even interface jacks. He was the magic man, the boy genius who had done more hacks before his fifteenth birthday than most runners manage in their entire careers. More importantly, he'd lasted through those difficult teen years without ever getting caught, transitioning from keyboards to interface jacks seamlessly while doing massive hacks that others only dreamed about. Though never prosecuted, many believed him to be behind the great 2021 Traffic Riot, a mega hack that caused all the traffic lights in the Los Angeles County area to malfunction at the same time, resulting in mass chaos. His legend had since grown to the point that only he could tell the difference between fact and the fictitious hyperbole of the GlobalNet rumor mill. A hacker's best advertisement was his reputation, and Freeman's reputation was beyond reproach.

Freeman had mostly retired from the public hacking scene during Bridge's early career. Everyone knew him, of course. His NetID had the same sort of cache as Timothy Leary among the drug culture. He could walk among hackers half his age and be revered as a god, despite the fact that he'd been working full-time for the Chronosoft Corporation for four years. Any other hacker who'd made the switch to regular nine-to-fiver would be labeled a sell-out, but not Michael Freeman. If anything, his reputation was a challenge to all the foolhardy runners out there, a bullseye painted on the Chronosoft databanks. If a hacker could pierce their security, it would mean they had bested Michael Fucking Freeman, god of hackers. Not that anyone ever did, of course. Freeman was just that good.

Bridge had one advantage over other runners wishing an audience with Freeman. He knew Angela. And he also knew that Angela had hired Freeman many times for jobs his corporate bosses would not have cleared. He could pick and choose the jobs, and Angela offered him the most challenging. Freeman liked Angela, or at least she thought he did. Bridge gambled that she was correct in her assumption, that Freeman would like her enough to help her out of a jam, even if that jam involved going up against Chronosoft.

Bridge found himself seated at a kitchen table in Freeman's downtown apartment. The late August sun made searing shapes on the worn linoleum of Freeman's kitchen. Unlike other runners, Freeman kept a meticulous home, every single object in its proper place. Bridge marveled at the order. It was painfully neat, everything lined up as if the owner had measured the distance between each object down to the millimeter, all arranged according to some intricately deranged plan.

"I hope I didn't wake you up," Bridge began as his coffee cooled.

Freeman shrugged it off. "I don't sleep much these days. The eggheads have me on some stuff I can't talk about." Freeman had the waxy skin of most crèche hackers, but his eyes lacked the telltale bags.

"They need help finding a distribution channel?" Bridge asked without thinking. Deals like that were just a reflex at this point.

Hooking up a black market distribution deal for cutting edge pharmas was big-time money. He had already started tallying percentages in his head when he caught a glimpse of Freeman's scowl.

"What happened to Angela, Bridge?" Freeman could not disguise his distaste for Bridge. They had met only once, and Freeman had not shown him much respect. Maybe it was the fact that his breakup with Angela had been ugly, maybe it was Bridge's line of work, or maybe he just didn't like ex-hackers. But that disdain had not changed. Freeman's elongated face punctuated by a scraggly goatee had disgust written all over it. "What did you get her into?"

"Whoa, whoa, I tried to keep her out of it. As a matter of fact, I told her specifically not to show up at the place. If she'd just stayed away, they wouldn't have been able to track me back to her apartment."

"Yeah, and you know Angela has always listened to what you said." Freeman laughed, but his smile was cold and humorless.

"Maybe you should explain what you were doing." Bridge sighed and relayed the whole story from start to finish. Freeman listened stoically, occasionally sipping his coffee and interrupting Bridge for clarification. "So you stumble across this recording, try to sell it and almost get yourself killed, and you expected Angela would just stay out of all that? Surely you aren't that dumb."

"Hey, I offered her a slice, and she didn't want to touch it. I thought she'd stay as far away from it as she possibly could, see if I could get myself capped trying to move the goods so she could laugh."

"Except you were in trouble, man. You got yourself into a big pile of trouble and it still surprises you that she came to your rescue. You really don't know her very well at all, do you?" He finished off a cup of coffee, and poured himself another from the carafe on the table.

"What do you mean?"

"What do I mean? What do you think I mean? I talked to her when you guys split up. You think she just jumped into bed with that fuckhead from Korea, don't you? Hell no. That girl was tore up. The only

eason she ever got with that Kim guy was because of his connections. She's been playing him from the getty. She's been holding a candle for you since the minute you left."

Bridge looked up from his cup quickly. "What? No, no, no. She threw ME out, didn't want me anywhere near her. Hell, she barely let me use any of her stable."

"If she really hated you like you thought, you think she'd have kept hooking you up? She treats those hackers like her children, and yet she hands them off to you for whatever shit you get them involved in. She's still looking out for you, whether you know it or not."

Bridge mulled it over. Maybe Freeman was right. Angela certainly had every opportunity to cut ties with Bridge any time she wished, and yet she hadn't. And now, she'd gotten herself in the thick of this mess over his objections, all because he'd put himself in a dangerous situation that would require rescue. "Shit, Freeman, she's a woman. I'm never going to be sure how she feels, and right now, it doesn't matter. It is what it is. These assholes have kidnapped her and I have to give them what they want."

"A leak? That's it?" Bridge nodded. "Seems like a lot of trouble for a leak.

So why call me? Leaks are script kiddie territory. It's not exactly a challenge. And who's to say they'll give her up even if you do what they say?"

Bridge smiled that smile, the one he used when he was working. It was the smile of supreme confidence, of the schemer putting his scheme into action. "That's where you come in. I got a plan." Bridge laid it all out for Freeman. The middle-aged hacker began to smile with each sentence, his smile getting bigger as the plan took shape. By the time Bridge was done, Freeman was positively beaming, his eyes twitching from side to side as he began to work out the details in his mind.

"I'm in," said Freeman. Bridge leaned back with a satisfied smile that hid the nervousness bubbling in the pit of his stomach.

Chapter 14
August 31, 2028
6:16 p.m.

The boiling afternoon sun was slowly sinking below the horizon as Bridge pulled Angela's rental into the guest garage of the downtown Chronosoft Civil Administration complex. Much of the massive, multi-building complex was still under construction, as an addition to the existing Chronosoft corporate headquarters. The crossover walkway between two of the buildings would not be finished for another six months, its skeletal framework casting eerie shadows on the ground. The building housing Thames' office was attached to the garage, its shiny exterior mostly completed though the upper six or so floors were still empty shells in need of final touch-ups. Another massive building that would eventually house all of the LGL's offices was nothing more than a girder skeleton projecting out of a dusty pit. Despite the late hour, hundreds of construction workers still toiled in the oppressive heat, Spanish curses mixed with English orders echoing from all areas. The droning, beeping blare of the warning claxons on heavy machinery dominated the scene. The sounds invaded the car as Bridge rolled down his window to the guard, who checked his credentials and directed Bridge to his parking place in excruciating detail. Security was excessively tight.

Bridge parked and prepared the car, removing all traces of anything he would need from the vehicle. He didn't expect to return to it no matter what happened. The walk to Thames' office was a long one, avoiding areas yet to be built and passing through multiple security checkpoints. Bridge was at least encouraged by the fact that Thames really was an entertainment division executive. Whatever political operation Bridge had been recruited into, it was at least being carried out far enough away from the elections division to be plausibly denied. Bridge admired the subterfuge.

Of course, he was made to wait outside the executive's office. It was a trick Bridge had used to his advantage many times. Despite the time frame Thames had set, he would be the one who would be calling the shots and setting the timetable. Thames would believe himself to be in control, and that was exploitable. Bridge shrugged and sat, watching the receptionist with a bemused smile that masked his nervousness. After a five-minute wait, one of Paulie's goons from this morning opened the office door and motioned Bridge in with a grunt. Bridge got up slowly, calmly taking his time in crossing the office.

"Come in, Mr. Bridge," Thames said, self-satisfied smugness dripping from his perfectly shaped mouth. Bridge really hated this guy now, but hid his disgust under a smarmy smile. "Sorry our meeting can't be under more congenial circum-stances, but you understand." He motioned to a chair in front of the oversized desk but Bridge preferred to remain standing. The office was a model in overcompensa-tion. Opulent white leather couches flanked the desk on both sides, a gigantic wall screen covered one wall and the desk was so large, it could serve two comfortably. The tiny chair Bridge had been directed to was dwarfed by the desk's girth, and Bridge assumed its position was meant to intimidate those who sat there. The wall screen ran a constant slideshow of various successful Chronosoft Entertainment properties. Thames sat behind the desk, leaning back comfortably in an almost throne-like office chair, its white leather so gaudy Bridge felt nauseous. Paulie's goons flanked either side of the desk in front of the floor-to-ceiling window. Paulie stood to the side of one of the couches, overseeing Angela, who sat cowed but openly hostile. The drug had worn off, and Bridge could see the mixture of fire and fear in her eyes.

"You all right, baby?" Bridge asked. She said nothing, only nodding with her jaw clenched so tight her teeth must have hurt. Bridge nodded back and winked at her, which only made her squint her eyes even tighter.

Turning his attention back to the smug douchebag in front of him, he said, "All right, jackhole, shall we do this thing?"

Thames looked offended. "Now, Mr. Bridge, is there really any need for hostility? I apologize for the violence, but you've been somewhat reluctant to comply. I mean, just look at what your friends did to Paulie over there." Paulie smiled the toothy grin of a predator. "We didn't want this kind of business, but then we chose badly on the front end. Kira's reputation as hardcore was vastly overinflated."

"He was a nice kid, you cocksucker!" Angela blurted. "If you'd come to me for this, I'd have given you somebody I knew could handle it. But you suits never fucking learn do you? You think everybody is just some replaceable..." Bridge cut her off with a wave of his arm.

"She got a point, you know. Hell, I'd have gotten you a better guy if you'd just come to me first. It's what I do."

Thames just shrugged. "Lesson learned, then. Have you done what we asked?"

"The leak? It's all set and ready to go." Bridge pulled out a bizchip. "All I have to do is activate this and we're off."

Thames tried to remain calm as he reached over the desk to grasp the chip, but his desperation showed through in his hurried motions. Bridge pulled the chip back. "Not so fast, there, Skippy. We've still got some unfinished business to discuss."

Paulie grabbed Angela by the throat, pulling her up off the couch with brutal strength. "There ain't no unfinished business here, Cupcake. Give the man the card and get on with it."

Thames was quick to chastise the heavy. "No, no, Paulie, no need for that. We don't want to get blood on my Persian there." He stared back at Bridge with bemused accommodation as Paulie released Angela. She gave the footballer a petulant slap on the ass and a look to curl the wallpaper. "What unfinished business exactly, Mr. Bridge?"

"Curiosity, mostly. See, I've been trying to figure this thing out. Here you've got an election, probably one of the biggest local elections in the country what with the Los Angeles LGL kind of being held up as the model for the entire national LGL program, right?" Thames nodded. "And your guy is throwing it. He's purposefully set himself up to lose this election. I don't doubt the peculiar virtual tastes he demonstrated for the recording are a regular thing for him, but he knew he was being recorded. He did it willingly, and you set the whole thing up for him. He didn't have very good things to say about you, by the way. Thought you were a bit too inexperienced for this sort of thing."

"His opinion really isn't relevant," Thames responded with mild annoyance.

"Yeah, I bet it isn't. What does he get out of it? What he did isn't illegal, but there aren't many people who want play-date pedophiles running their city. This gets out, especially this close to the election, and the only thing people will think of in the voting booth is whether to pick the good-looking anti-corporate crusader or the fatass pedobear. His career is finished."

"Indeed. Mr. Sunderland is well aware of his situation. But as you've pointed out, he's done nothing illegal. He can retire to some out of the way place to do whatever he wishes. His name will be mud, but if he can take a few months' public roasting, his future is assured. He'll never have to work again. With the fickle nature of the public, the story might not even last one news cycle. He retires rich, which is really all he cared about. He wasn't exactly a willing civil servant in the first place."

"So why pick him? Was he always going to be a fall guy?"

Thames seemed to mull this over for a moment, as if trying to decide just how much he should bother to tell Bridge. He could have stopped at any time, but as he began to speak again, Bridge knew he couldn't resist. He was damn proud of whatever this plan was and he couldn't resist a good brag. "Of course. Despite what our press relations department is saying publicly, the LGL is not exactly popular with the masses. Selling the concept was always going to be difficult, no matter how bad the riots were. We needed someone to be 'our guy,' the corporate mouthpiece."

"And you needed the opposite," Bridge finished both his thought and Thames's at the same time. "You needed a protagonist, a hero for the masses, the crusader against the big bad corporation. Your movie needed a good guy."

Thames nodded enthusiastically. The executive was thoroughly impressed with himself. "Exactly. That's the trick we've learned about democracy, you see. Democracy is inherently chaotic, with the will of the people often easily swayed by all sorts of externalities, things like fear and pride and greed. But if you can control those externalities, manipulate those factors, democracy is imminently control-lable."

"But if you wanted Soto for mayor, why not just fudge the votes? You control the voting machines, the voting process, all of it. Why not just control the count?"

"Too easy to track. Besides, the masses have spent decades mistrusting the counts anyway. While it puts our chosen man into position, it makes people sus-picious of his administration. Did he really win? Was it just some shenanigans behind the scenes?

However, if you infect his opponent with scandal, if you make the choice be-tween candidates the choice between good and evil, the masses will be behind him completely. They'll give him more leeway to do things they'd never support other-wise." Thames was excited now, leaning forward across the desk with the smile of a child displaying his refrigerator masterpiece. "You see, control isn't enough.

Controlling the masses overtly just creates ill will. An iron glove is resented. You have to give the masses the illusion of control. Let them think they've made the choice you want them to make and you can lead them anywhere you wish. They will follow you gladly. By the time anyone really figures out your game, it won't matter because they've already given you what you wanted."

"And Soto? He's in on it?"

"Certainly. Who do you think is building this complex?" Thames pointed out the window at the massive frame of the construction next door. "He stands to make a lot of money from this deal, through all sorts of proxies, of course. He deserves an Oscar for his turn as the working man's hero in this little picture but he's hardly a saint. The things he did during the riots could land him in jail for life."

"All of which disappears if he just goes along with this little game?" Thames nodded again.

"It's the Algebra of Need, Mr. Bridge," the smarmy suit replied.

"William Burroughs. Nice. A bit before your time, though isn't it?"

"And yours. I'm impressed. I didn't realize you were that well-read."

"You'd be amazed what I've read, Mr. Thames. And me? Why involve me?"

"Your connections. Once Kira went off the reservation, we had to find some way to get to him, and your connection with Angela was the best we could find on short notice. She's not exactly easy for someone like me to approach."

"Yeah, I have a douchebag detector installed," Angela said.

"Artie's is broken."

"Does that satisfy your curiosity, Mr. Bridge? No more useless questions then?" Bridge shook his head. "Then will you please do what we've asked? I have eight o'clock dinner reservations at Spago."

Bridge held out the bizchip. "If you'd care to do the honors?"

Thames reached for the card quickly, but a thought stopped him cold. He put up his hands as if the card was a gun. "No, that's all I need is for you to capture my fingerprints on the transaction and use it against me."

Bridge frowned. "Really? I get that little trust? Fine, I'll do it myself." He grabbed the bizchip with his other hand, activating the program that started the leak. "Besides, if I really wanted your fingerprints on this operation, I have more than enough DNA off of your other cards to do what I would need." Thames face sank a bit. "Don't worry, I didn't. I hate blackmail. It's more trouble than it's worth."

"So it's done then?"

Bridge nodded. "Give it six hours, and every body who's anybody in the underground news, blogging and political scene will have published, dissected and bloviated on the video at length. It should hit the morning news cycle like a freight train, just in time for the masses' morning coffee before going off to the voting booths."

"Well if that's all..." Thames began, throwing a glance towards Paulie, who nodded knowingly.

"Not so fast," Bridge interrupted. Paulie's hand, which had been moving towards his jacket, stopped suddenly. "You got your leak. But with a situation such as we find ourselves in here, I couldn't take the chance that your boy Paulie over here wouldn't just whack the two of us once you got what you wanted. So I gave myself a little insurance."

Thames' jaw set and he asked through clenched teeth, "What kind of insurance?"

Bridge threw the bizchip down on the desk, where it began to immediately smoke and dissolve. "Don't worry, you got your untraceable leak. The leak contained a little something something, a little extra if you will. A very well-hidden trojan."

The pompous executive's faced dropped, his eyes narrowing in a burning glance. "What does it do?" Thames' voice was laced with angry impatience.

"Nothing much. It just attacks the voting machines, the election commission's network. Those voting counts you don't want to manipulate? I just did."

"Those counts are secured..." Thames' voice trailed off as he started to realize the implications.

"Seriously? You're going to count on the machines you yourself claim can be manipulated easily. You're going to count on those things' security? You said it yourself, manipulating the ballots are too easy to track, and as soon as the press gets wind those counts are suspect, there goes your election. If the process itself isn't trusted, neither is your candidate."

Thames had the look of shocked defeat plastered across his mug. All trace of his former smugness was gone. "That kind of hack would take more than you've got," he said, but his confidence was shaky.

Bridge smiled. "You're right." He motioned to Angela, who quickly got up to join him. "But I know a guy." Bridge's smile got even wider, an infuriatingly toothy grin. He began to back away towards the door. Paulie looked towards Thames for orders then back at Bridge and back at the executive again, unsure of what to do. "Now I see I've confused the Limey Ape over here, but I'm sure you get the gist of what I'm telling you."

"What do you want?"

"I'm pretty cheap, actually. You let us go, alive and leave us that way for three months. Three months is all I ask. Keep the ape off me for that long, and you'll get the code to clear this whole thing up."

"Three months? We need that election settled tomorrow night."

"And I need to keep breathing for three months. This isn't a negotiation, Mr.

143

Thames. Three months. Or you can just kill us now and sort out the counts when you get them sorted out. Do we have a deal?"

Thames pondered it for only a second, before agreeing with a sigh. "We have a deal."

"Smart man." He turned around, ushering Angela out the door quickly, then paused. Bridge turned back to Thames and said, "You know, you could have saved us all some time if you'd just come to me in the beginning. Shit, I don't give a fuck if you elect Mickey Goddamn Mouse if you pay me enough to set the whole thing up. But you had to get cute. You had to fuck with me. You had to fuck with her. You want something from me you come at me straight up. Maybe next time you'll know better than to fuck with me."

"Don't cross the Bridge?" Thames asked with sarcastic amusement.

"Not unless you're willing to pay the toll," Bridge responded all too aware how corny that sounded. "Now fuck off, you cunt." Bridge slammed the door behind him.

"Let's not dawdle, my dear," Bridge said to Angela. He led her away from the elevators and down the stairs. "No, no, we're not taking the car. It won't be useable anyway."

"What did you do to my rental?"

"Yeah, it's not your rental anymore. Thames just bought himself a soon-to-be burned out husk of a rental sedan," Bridge said with a smile. They almost ran down the stairs and out the back, cutting across side streets to catch a bus that almost left them at the curb. Bridge had his escape route all planned. The car would have combusted right about the time they reached the street, and as they boarded the bus, he could already hear the wailing screech of the garage's fire alarm.

"He is going to be so pissed," she said with that mischievous grin.

"Especially after you fucked up his election."

"Oh that. Well, not exactly."

"What do you mean? That's what you bought our lives with, what do you mean not exactly?"

"Well, I didn't technically hack the ballot. It's sure going to look like I tried, and it'll take them months to figure out that nothing was altered. Months and months and months and millions of dollars and most importantly, all that trust they were hoping Soto would have as mayor. Whoever gets elected tomorrow, it'll be a clean count, at least as far as my efforts are concerned. But damn is it going to be painful to figure that out." Bridge was beaming.

"You risked our lives on a bluff?" He nodded vigorously. "You motherfucker. You absolute cocksucker. That is the most brilliant hack I've ever seen."

"Ain't it though? See, there's some use to being a manipulative cocksucker."

Her dour scowl dissolved into a lascivious grin. "I've got a use for you when we get home, you rat bastard." She gave him a long kiss. When she had detached herself, she looked around the bus with an embarrassed self-consciousness.

"Tomorrow, we look for a new place."

"We?" He arched an eyebrow at her.

"You just put us on the shit list of the biggest LGL on the West Coast. We're joined at the hip, you and me. Might be a good idea if we disappear off their radar for a bit." Bridge nodded agreement and leaned back into his seat. Three months wasn't a long time, but it would have to do.

Epilogue
October 31, 2028
7:22 p.m.

The next two months were eventful for Bridge and Angela. True to her word, she moved them in together that week, refusing to take no for an answer as she and Bridge abandoned their respective apartments in the middle of the night.

A creative use of some of her best freelance credcrashers saw their leases dissolved, their belongings packed up as quietly as possible and shifted from apartment to storage space, where another application of the hacking arts caused those goods to disappear.

It was an expensive move, as far as Bridge could tell, but Angela handled most of it and either footed the bill or had someone else pay for it without their knowledge. Bridge laid low for the week after the election, rescheduling as many of his appointments as he could. He lost a few jobs, but nothing he couldn't replace once he felt a bit safer.

The election was a colossal slow-motion train wreck, of course. As Bridge had predicted, the Sunderland story took off. The first downloads happened within minutes of Bridge's exit from Chronosoft headquarters, and by morning, it had over 100,000 views. The news networks, freed from their gag order by the underground release, swooped in on the story like ravenous vultures. An estimated 85% of all Los Angeles LGL eligible voters were said to have seen the recording or heard about the recording from a news outlet or friend. Only hours after voting began, with exit polls showing Soto riding a burgeoning landslide, Freeman's hacking became apparent. Voting machines began to malfunction, hiccup or otherwise show signs of irregularities and in a panic, the election commissioner tried to shut the voting booths down city-wide, beginning in some of the neighborhoods hardest hit by the riots. With resentment still simmering from the riots, the people reacted just as one would expect them to react when the corporate-controlled government attempted to disenfranchise them. Riots were only narrowly avoided. While there were some injuries and property damage, the efficiency of CLED negotiators averted a repeat of the previous year's violence. In the end, the election commissioner decided to let the vote go ahead as scheduled. By the time the polls had closed, the rout was obvious. Soto had won, but the media cast a pall on the victory party by reporting on the voting machine irregularities and near-riots. Days were spent with the election commissioner on the hot seat, with both parties clamoring for certification, reporters requesting an investigation and rumors flying. By the end of the week, the commissioner had resigned in disgrace and the election was certified by his successor, triggering disenfranchisement lawsuits and rendering Soto's enormous victory tainted. Bridge never had so much fun watching the news feeds.

His reunion with Angela was not always as entertaining. There were many marathon-length talking sessions, heartfelt discussions about their feelings and shrieking arguments. Through it all,

however, neither gave in and more importantly, neither gave up on the relationship. Something in the months they'd spent apart and in the crazy day they'd spent almost dying together had forged a stronger bond between the two. Angela still disliked the way he made his money. "You're not an amoral bastard, you know," she said at one point. "You just know how to push your few principles aside to deal with the scum of the earth. What I don't get is how you can stand to deal with them."

Finally, he'd explained it as best he could. "Look, I know these people are shit. I get the worst of the worst. I don't get little old ladies who need me to get their pension back from the loan shark. I get the loan shark when he needs a new guy to break the little old lady's legs. And I help him, and you know why I help him? Leave aside the fact that even if I refuse to help him, someone else will. That's just a fact. I help him because I know that guy is going down a one-way road the wrong way. And eventually, some other dumb fucker is going to come down that road from the opposite direction. So I just run them both into each other so the sorry bastards can get themselves the fuck off my planet sooner."

Angela laughed and shook her head. "Bullshit. That's bullshit. You're trying to rationalize the fact that you make money off of misery because you gotta eat. It's not some kind of twisted service to the world."

"Maybe. We all gotta eat. But I'd rather those guys eat each other than me." And nothing more was said about it.

Gina Danton had gotten Aristotle off the charge, just as she had promised. With the mayor's greatly reduced respectability in those first hours of election day, no one had given two shits that Aristotle had pulled his mischief at the mayor's fundraiser, not when a cop of Danton's reputation had been willing to vouch for the bodyguard. Amazingly, Aristotle never gave Bridge any grief over his arrest, instead making light of it as often as he could. Bridge still ended up buying the giant a fantastically bejeweled watch, making sure to show it off to Angela before giving the gift.

Nicky took care of himself. Bridge had set up the bust with Danton, of course, and Bridge spent a few good hours worrying that the Cajun mobster would evade capture and come directly after Bridge. Nicky, never the sharpest tool in the shed, decided instead to go out Tony Montana style, trying to shoot his way out of the dragnet. He did manage to wound one cop before getting perforated. Thinking back on it, Bridge felt no remorse for his part in the gangster's death. Nicky was too stupid too live, too selfish to remove himself from the gene pool and too worthless to feel any guilt over. Nicky's guys drifted from one boss to another, like all hard guys do. None of them had the talent or brains to make much of themselves beyond hired muscle.

Paulie was a problem, of course. Soon after Bridge started working again, Paulie became a regular fixture at all the spots where Bridge plied his trade. Bridge would be finishing up work with a client when he'd spy the ex-footballer standing at the bar, eyes burning holes through Bridge. Paulie would spot Bridge, Bridge would spot Paulie and the heavy would raise his new cybernetic hand in a sarcastic salute. Before leaving, Paulie would point the cyberhand at Bridge and make the sign of a pistol with his thumb and first two fingers, then exit with that same predatory smile of his. Short of hiring someone to whack the footballer, Bridge really hadn't come up with a good way to deal with that grudge, but he still had a month to go.

A month was a long time. Hell, Bridge could get hit by a bus in that month. He could get abducted by aliens, or blown up along with half a city. Some punk ass disgruntled client could come back and stick a vibroknife in his back. He'd figure something out when the time came. That was what he did best. He figured things out. He'd figured out the Sunderland mess, and stuck it to "the man" in the process. Paulie wasn't nearly as smart as Thames. And if he couldn't figure something out, well, he knew a guy that could.

FIN

FEEDING AUTONOMY

The following is a short story that takes place months before the event depicted in this novel.

"They said you were the guy to talk to about special requests." Bridge put on as devious a grin as he could, but the revulsion he felt when listening to this weedy frat boy talk was difficult to tamp down. Bridge had done his usual due diligence on potential clients. The little douche sitting across the circular booth was named

Conner Archer, eldest son of some upper middle manager at Chronosoft, Inc. His daddy made good bank in software, and as a result, the kid got to fuck off at UCLA with as much beer, weed, Trip and whatever else he could shove down his rapacious gullet without fear of expulsion. Bridge hated everything about the kid; his spiky blond hair, his weasel grin, the erratic way he waved his hands around as he ran his mouth. The two kids to either side were just as irritating. One was a muscular jock type, a track and field kid whose father was an account executive at Chronosoft's local news division. The third kid was a wannabe. His parents were struggling middle class, and the only way he'd managed to make it into both UCLA and the frat was because his daddy was an alumnus. He seemed to be trying way too hard to impress his more well-heeled brothers.

Bridge went through the usual routine. He asked if they were cops, or if they were wired, even though his white noise generator would have killed any attempts to eavesdrop on the conversation. Then he explained his services. "You need some-thing, I know somebody got that something. You stand over here looking for some-thing and the guy with that something is across the river over there. I'm the Bridge between you."

"What river?" asked the middle-class kid, Brett.

"It's metaphorical. Try to keep up. For a nominal fee, I will find you that guy and hook you up. I don't make judgements and I don't ask questions. I don't touch nothing and I don't know nothing. I'm all about the connection, the circuit. You tell me, I tell him and nobody else. Now, what is this special request?"

"We want some Sluv," Archer said with a devious grin. "A whole bunch."

Bridge nodded. Sluv, the new nanotech designer date rape drug. Forget Roofies, or Spanish fly or any of that other shit, Sluv was the new hotness. Spanish fly was dangerous in the hands of complete imbeciles like these and results couldn't be guaranteed. Roofies made the girls comatose. The old standby of getting chicks drunk too often led to passed out broads or Woo Girls throwing up all over the intended rapist. Sluv, though, Sluv were a sure thing. It messed with both the decision-making and memory centers of the brain. The victim became almost hypnotically suggestible; tell the chicks to blow an entire football team and they would do it without resistance. The drug altered their memories of the events, making them believe every act they'd taken had been their choice. It even played well with alcohol and other drugs, almost eliminating the danger of an adverse reaction. It flushed itself from the system in 24-hours, making it untraceable. If the rapist could afford the premium, he could have his way with whomever he wanted and get away clean.

The chestnut-haired twerp next to Archer, Sal Pearson, explained their request. "We got this big-time New Year's Eve Party coming up," he rubbed his hands together, "and we got some major hottie action invited. We want to make sure the brothers get their pick of the litter, know what I mean?"

154

Bridge kept that smile on his face, tossing the kid a conspiratorial wink. "Say no more." He stopped as the punks giggled like schoolgirls. "No, really, say no more. I don't need nor want to know what you use the product for. You never knew me and I never knew you, got it? I know a guy. You give me 24 hours and I'll have you a meeting set up. My cut is $3,000 in advance. You pay in cash, five-year, deposited in a locker at this address. We meet tomorrow night and I'll give you the details."

"You could tell us some bullshit and leave us hanging!" the middle-class kid, Brett Wolf, said. "Uh uh, you get paid after we get our stuff."

Bridge got serious. He could see the gigantic form of his bodyguard, Aristotle, hovering over him in the mirrored wall behind his clients. He gave the bodyguard a subtle hand signal to keep the giant from interfering. "That isn't how it works. You may not know me, but you know of me, right? And do you really think anybody would have given you my name if I was the kind to fuck over a client? No, they wouldn't because I'm not. My word is bond. I tell you you'll get the meet, get it you will. Whether you can work out a deal is your problem, not mine. People use my services because I know people they don't, and I don't give a fuck what it is you want or how you are going to use it because it never touches my hands. I do nothing illegal. Now if you want to go wandering around asking people for highly illegal drugs because you're too cheap or paranoid to use me, we'll see where that gets you. But if you want your drugs, I can save you the trouble of getting guns stuck in your face for asking very dangerous people very dangerous questions. We clear?"

The three exchanged nervous glances. Archer tossed an angry bug-eyed stare at Wolf, which seemed to silence him. "No, it's cool, man. You're the guy we want to deal with. Here's my card." He handed Bridge a flashy bizchip. "Call me when you have things set up. You'll get your money." Bridge chuckled inside at the uselessness of a college kid with a bizchip, but took it without comment.

"You won't be disappointed, young gents," Bridge said with the biggest shit-eating grin he could muster.

"You're going to do what?"

Angela's tone was bitingly chilly, malicious anger bleeding through her voice despite the crèche's tinny speaker. Bridge's live-in girlfriend, Angela Powell, was jacked into the GlobalNet, an architect of a number of massive virtual worlds and full-time information broker for a stable of hackers domestic and international. Bridge used to be one of them, before the riots last August. The experiences the two of them had shared during those awful days had affected them both in different ways. While Bridge had given up the hacker life and become the know-to, go-to guy, the amoral fixer with the slick patter, Angela had retreated deeper into the GlobalNet. Their apartment, never the most well-kept joint, had become an absolute shithole. Used food containers and dirty dishes were left everywhere, dust accumulated on every surface, dirty clothes piled up in the closets and hallways, towels mildewed on the bathroom floor when Bridge neglected to pick them up. Angela didn't see the mess most days anyway. She spent hours and days at a stretch buried in the coffin-like crèche. The layer of dust coating its exterior dulled the shiny black surface, but it was the only thing Bridge ever saw of her anymore.

"I gotta get some Sluv for a bunch of fratboys," he repeated flatly. "What's Doc Cramer's number, babe?"

"What am I, your fucking yellow pages? Look it up yourself, asshole."

Bridge raised an eyebrow. "I take it you don't approve."

The speaker was silent for long, tense moments. The silent treatment then. Bridge sighed and went to his own abandoned crèche, similarly dusty. He brought up the exterior console and began a search for Cramer's number. "You're just going to ignore me?" Bridge sighed again.

"Ignore what? You didn't say anything."

"You shouldn't even have to ask me if I approve. You're getting a date rape drug for a bunch of leg-humping rich boy cocksuckers."

"Of course. The leg-humping poor boy cocksuckers aren't profitable."

"How can you even look at yourself in the mirror? They are going to rape some drunk college bow bitch and you're going to give them the stuff so they can get away with it. You might as well be raping them yourself!"

Bridge had found Cramer's number and transferred it to his internal HUD. "Don't be so fucking dramatic. You know as well as I do these fuckheads would rape a lamppost if they could get it drunk enough. It isn't like they need the drug to bang some sorority chick against her will. They could get her drunk, or just beat her into submission. At least with this shit, the chick isn't likely to get a beatdown."

"Wow, you miserable fuck. That's the most sickening rationalization I've ever heard in my life. What the fuck happened to you?"

The old argument had cycled back around again like some ravenous beast, never satisfied with tiny nibbles at their relationship. The same arguments, the same justifications, the same insults, they always returned, each time with more anger, more venom and more hurtful words that couldn't be taken back. Angela had resented his choices, had resented his leaving behind the hacking life. Though she had been in charge of the illegal information brokering business, as their relationship had grown closer, he had taken a good deal of the responsibility from her shoulders, and he was a fantastic organizer. His absence had hurt her professionally, but she took it personally, as if he had repudiated her entirely.

At her best, Angela was not a social person, at least not in the flesh. She was not the most attractive person. Her gangly arms, small breasts and crooked teeth hardly matched the accepted version of good-looking. Bridge knew her self-image was terrible, but when she tried, she was much prettier than she believed herself to be. The fact that Bridge had been able to shift from the virtual to the meat world with very little adjustment must have stirred a jealousy she didn't even want to acknowledge.

Bridge had earned the nickname the Amoral Bridge by being exactly that. He didn't care what his clients wanted him to find, what depravity they requested, what immoral acts they wished to perform. The client wanted it and he got it, no questions asked. His only request was that whatever illegal service or product got exchanged never touch him. All he did was connect the buyer with the seller. That couldn't be illegal, or at least not illegal enough to get him much heat. That amorality was another sticking point with Angela, despite her chosen profession.

"How do you help these shitheels do these things without throwing up? Don't they disgust you?"

Bridge exploded. He'd heard it all so many times by now that he was sick to the death of it all. "They all disgust me, every fucking one of them! All of them! EVERYBODY! You think I go out of my way to find these people, that I have to look hard for clients? Shit. I have to turn people away some days, not because I give two flying fucks what they want, but because I just don't have the time. You think there's normal people out there that don't want nasty shit like virtual videos of their friends getting tortured, or hired killers, or kidnappers, or date rape drugs but there ain't. Everybody wants to do something nasty and vile to somebody else. Everybody! They're all fucking shitheels with disgusting, immoral, vicious desires buried in their tiny, miserable souls just waiting for an excuse to get out. The sooner it gets out and they all burn themselves up in a fiery orgy of self-destructive gluttony, the happier I'll be. Humanity as a whole is a miserable gaggle of self-pleasuring apes ready to crack you over the head and steal your fucking bananas."

Having found the number, he felt trapped, closed into a slowly shrinking box that was their apartment. The air was stuffy and smelled of rotten food. He needed to get out, needed space and air. He couldn't take it anymore. He would head down to the club and call Cramer. He would set the whole thing up and be done with these bastards.

"That's it, I'm done. Fuck you, Bridge. If you do this, I'm done." Her words echoed through the hallway as he shuffled quickly towards the door.

"Then I guess you're fucking done," he said as the slammed the door.

"And you're sure this guy is solid?" Archer whined. His rat-faced grin, so smug and self-assured gave Bridge the urge to plant a quick jab right on the guy's pointy nose, an urge he fought down with some difficulty.

"Doc Cramer is a hundred percenter," Bridge replied with no hint of malice in his voice. "Whatever he sells you will be the mad notes."

"It better be," Pearson threatened, "or we will bury you."

"You know, I got plenty of business from people who don't threaten me. Maybe I should go take care of some of it." Bridge was genuinely ready to walk away, if for no other reason than to see how far they'd go to get him back. If he pushed it, if they really tried to play the hardass, he might even be able to get a few extra points out of the deal. Bridge started to stand, and Archer almost knocked the table over to keep him from leaving. Aristotle had tired of the game and leaned over the back of their booth, exposing his tree-trunk thick biceps to full view. Archer thought better of actually touching Bridge once he saw the dark form of the bodyguard hovering over the transaction.

"Sal, shut the fuck up, dude. I got this. It's cool, man. It's all good. We're all friends here." Archer couldn't take his eyes off the bodyguard's arms.

Bridge sat back down, his smile oozing smug triumph. "If the dick-measuring contest is quite through with, let's get down to business." He pulled a bizchip from his pocket and laid it in the exact center of the table. "Payment received, so we're all set on my end. You put your thumb on this chip and Cramer will contact you shortly to set up fulfillment. I never see the stuff, and I never met you. You can back out now, and I'll refund half the fee and we never met." Bridge had to give them the out, give them the opportunity to tamp down their worst desires. He was always surprised when someone took that opportunity, mostly because it was such a rare occurrence. Despite the profit, he was always a little disappointed when a deal went through. But the more jobs he did, the more he saw that the people who sought him couldn't help themselves, no matter how self-destructive their requests were, no matter how far down the path to self-immolation they already were. His

160

clients either couldn't help themselves or didn't want to.

Archer giggled with depraved glee and jammed his thumb down onto the card. It flashed twice. Bridge picked it up and tossed it into the sparkling clean ashtray where it smoked and shriveled before catching fire and dissolving into a fine pile of ash. "Enjoy your party, boys," Bridge said and waved them off. They left with hardy back slaps and effervescent excitement.

Despite the fee, Bridge was going to make nothing on this job. He had traded his entire fee to Cramer for a special request of his own. Bridge knew that his reputation required that he get his fratboys exactly what they wanted no matter how sleazy it made him feel. But their attitude towards him demanded attention. There was no reason to be so dickish in business. He could have gotten them anything they wanted and looked the other way without blinking, but they had to play the alpha male. Spoiled rich kids with nothing to lose because their daddy's money would always backstop any bad behavior really pissed him off. So he asked Cramer to work a little extra magic on his client's order of Sluv.

The drugs would work, of course. They could dissolve it in a chick's drink, or place the paper-thin tabs on the girl's skin. Within minutes, the victim would be completely suggestible, a fully conscious robot awaiting whatever depraved instructions the boys could dream up. The men would touch the tabs since Sluv were normally designed to only work on female body chemistry. Unfortunately for Archer and his would-be rapists, Bridge had asked Cramer to spike the dose.

The rapists would get their victims, but they'd be completely impotent for the entire duration. Whether the male touched the tab to administer the drug, or touched the victim's skin after it took effect, there was a second nano component that turned a male's equipment into a flaccid noodle.

Bridge was taking a chance, of course. The disappointed customers might try to blame Bridge, but to do that, they'd have to admit they couldn't close the deal. Bridge was betting on the fragile ego of the alpha male. If there was one thing Bridge figured he could count on, it was his client's inability to admit they couldn't lay pipe at a moment's notice. They would lie to each other, maybe even lie to themselves, but the odds they would put two and two together to equal Bridge were astronomical. It may have cost Bridge his entire fee, but it was worth it.

Bridge thought about Angela with a scowl darkening his face. Angela had made her arrangements moments after he slammed the door. His shit would be gone by the time he returned. He thought briefly about calling her, about trying to explain what he'd done, but dismissed it. He could explain all he wanted, but the distance between them had grown too wide, had grown with every job he'd done, with every minute he'd spent doing this thing he had to do.

ABOUT THE AUTHOR

Gary A. Ballard was born, raised and still resides in the state of Mississippi. He began writing at the age of 11, completing a number of really bad, thankfully un-published novels during his teen years. Graduating from Belhaven College with a degree in Fine Arts, he has painted, photographed, drawn, and written the world as he sees it. Working as a web designer since the early days of the World Wide Web, Gary is well-versed in social media, graphic design and Internet marketing. He currently lives with his wife and three insane dogs, and updates his personal blog, The Game of Angst, found at gameangst.blogspot.com and The Bridge Chronicles Blog, found at amoralbridge.blogspot.com.

Made in the USA
Middletown, DE
03 January 2015